SECRET SANTA

SECRET SERIES
BOOK 10

JILL SANDERS

To Nancy
May this next year
have fewer knives in it.

This is a work of fiction. Names, characters, places, and incidents either are the product of the author's imagination or are used fictitiously, and any resemblance to actual persons, living or dead, business establishments, events or locales is entirely coincidental.

ISBN: 978-1-945100-62-8

PRINT ISBN: 9798831932683

Print ISBN:

Copyeditor: Erica Ellis – inkdeepediting.com

SUMMARY

Kara is eager to show her father that she's capable of running the family's ranch in Wyoming. When her dad and stepmother head out on a three-month European tour, she eagerly takes the reins. Her only problem? Her annoying neighbor has decided that he's more fit for the job.

Nick has lived next to Kara all his life. Having a secret crush on the sexy brunette has taken a toll on his life. When his father falls ill and tells him the family ranch will be sold unless Nick finds a bride before Christmas, he knows just who he's always wanted. The only problem is persuading Kara that he's the right man for her.

PROLOGUE

Nicholas Howe the third was in love. This time, he was pretty sure it was the real deal. But what did an eight-year-old know of love?

As the pretty brunette girl stormed towards him, her long braids laid over her shoulders, he was absolutely positive this was the last time he'd fall in love.

"What do you think you're doing?" The girl glared up at him.

"Ridin'," he answered quickly, wanting to impress the girl. After all, he'd climbed on Hunter, one of his father's horses, all by himself and had taken off to ride the fence lines. A man's job.

His ranch had been in the Howe family for four generations. At least it would be when he finally inherited the land.

"I can see you're riding," the girl answered, putting extra emphases on the 'ing' in the word. His pa never corrected him, even though his teachers did. "Why are you here?" The girl motioned to the stand of trees Nick had stopped to rest under. There was a creek that went by them, and Hunter was drinking from the cold clean water.

"I'm just resting my horse," Nick answered, giving Hunter a pat on the neck for show. "What are you doing here?"

Instead of answering, the girl glared at him.

"This is my creek," she finally said.

"Yours?" Nick's dark eyebrows rose. "I don't think so. It's on my land," he said, feeling a lick of anger for the first time.

"Your land?" The girl laughed.

Nick glanced over to where her pony was tied to a low branch of the tree. It stood watching them.

"Yup, you're on Howe land," he answered proudly. "But I'll let you and your lame pony rest here for a while if you want."

The girl stopped laughing. "Lilly isn't..." She shook her head. "She isn't lame." She frowned up at him.

"She's not a horse." He patted Hunter again. "Not like Hunter here."

The girl crossed her arms over her chest and stuck out her bottom lip in a cute pout. Nick enjoyed it, but he didn't know why.

"You're too small to be riding a big horse like that." The girl looked up and shielded her eyes from the sun to see him better.

"You're too big to be riding such a small one," he pointed out.

The girl's face grew red. "Who are you?"

He smiled. "Nicholas James Howe the third," he said, using his full name to make himself sound more important. "Who are you?"

"Kara," she answered.

"Kara what?"

"Montgomery," she answered. "My dad, Carl Montgomery, just purchased this land, along with our house." She motioned behind her to the ranch home that sat at the base of a small hill.

"Then we're neighbors," he said, motioning behind him. "My family has owned Howe Ranch for four generations." He pointed to his home in the distance.

The girl frowned and was quiet for a while. "You're still on my land."

He smiled. "Nope, you're on mine. Now, if you'll excuse me, I think Hunter is done drinking."

He picked up Hunter's reins and tried to turn the massive horse back towards his barn, but the horse jerked its head, almost sending Nick falling forward over the horse's neck.

"I told you, you're too small for a horse that size," Kara said, crossing her arms over her chest again.

"Am not," he said, letting his pride get the better of him. He pulled on the reins again, but Hunter was having nothing of it. He jerked back and stomped his hoof and snorted.

"Hunter," he scolded, "let's go back home." He jerked again, and Hunter shook his entire body and lunged to the side. Nick hadn't been expecting the move and, in one quick motion, he slipped off the side of the horse and landed in the mud directly at Kara's feet. Hunter used his new freedom to sprint across the field, heading directly towards the barn.

His dad was going to skin him, he thought as he watched the back end of the horse. Then he glanced up and saw Kara smiling down at him.

"Told ya." She climbed on her pony and gracefully rode

back to her house while laughing at him.

CHAPTER ONE

Ten years later...

Nick got jerked around as he held onto the bull. Kara would have screamed, but the horror of what she was seeing had caused her voice to seize up. Instead, her fingers gripped the wood fence tighter as she silently prayed and counted the seconds.

When the buzzer sounded, he gracefully slid off the bull's back and hopped onto the railing of the fence, a few feet from her. He had the gall to wink at her as he climbed over the rungs and landed directly at her feet.

"So, what'd ya think?" he asked her, shifting his black Stetson further onto his head.

"I think..." she started, feeling her heart still racing, and not from watching him ride the bull, "that you're an idiot." She turned on her heels and stormed back to her seat next to her dad.

"That kid's got more guts than brains," her father said

under his breath.

"Yeah," she agreed.

"I think it was wonderful," Luanna said.

Kara's mother had died shortly before Kara turned eight, before they'd moved to Wyoming from California. It had taken years before her father had started dating again. Two crazy women later, he'd met Luanna while they'd been on a vacation in Hawaii. One short year later, after a very long-distance courtship, he'd married her and given Kara an older stepbrother, Beau, whom Kara adored. She adored both of them, actually—mother and son.

Beau had joined the military after graduating from high school. Then, he'd moved back to Hawaii to be closer to his roots. Kara and her family visited him often.

Kara watched Nick move back over to where the rest of the riders stood waiting for their turn in the spotlight. Their mere seconds of glory. When she noticed Nick watching her, she jerked her eyes away.

"He sure has grown up," her father said. "I remember when he was barely big enough to climb on a horse himself."

Kara remembered the day she'd met Nick and smiled. It was the one time she could hold over him. The one time he hadn't been... smooth. Since then, he'd proved over and over that he belonged in the saddle. Including bull riding now, apparently.

For the next hour, she sat and watched the riders come and go. When she got hungry, she made her way to the snack bar and had just ordered herself a burger when someone gripped her waist from behind.

"There you are, Kara."

Kara groaned. "What do you want, Willy?" she said without looking at the boy behind her.

"My name is Wil," he said tersely. "I wanted to make sure you watched me ride. So you could imagine what it'd feel like when I take you." Willy bumped his hips against her butt. She jerked forward and pushed him away.

"Gross," she said, shoving him again. "That is never going to happen."

Willy smiled and tried to pull her close again, locking her hips against his.

Several people waiting in line watched them, but no one did anything about it. Willy and his dad, Wilbert, were the town bullies, and no one wanted to cross them.

Kara fought him off as best as she could without punching him square in the jaw. Even though he was good-looking, probably one of the hottest guys in her class, he was a perve and an ass.

"Leave me be," she finally said, shoving him again. Somehow she miscalculated and ended up in his arms again.

"Is there a problem?" someone said directly behind them.

Kara groaned inwardly. Nick and Willy were mortal enemies and cousins. Whatever Willy did, Nick did it better and usually with more grace. However good-looking Willy was, Nick was easily twice that.

"Leave us alone, Nick," Willy said. Somehow Willy always managed to make Nick's name come out like a curse.

"Kara, I came to tell you that your folks are leaving. They asked if I could give you a ride home. That is, if you wanted to stay longer," Nick suggested.

Kara jerked free from Willy's hold when her order finally came up. She grabbed her burger and thought about leaving.

She'd promised her best friend Liz she'd watch her

barrel racing, which was after the bull rides.

"Thanks," she told Nick. Then she glared at Willy as she followed Nick back to the stands.

"You know, if you'd tell Willy you're not interested..." Nick started.

Kara jerked to a stop. "I've told Willy so many times over the years to leave me alone." She practically yelled it.

Nick looked embarrassed for a split second. "Right, I only meant—"

"Piss off." She started walking again, but Nick easily caught up with her. He was so damn tall and had very long legs. Legs that had filled in with strong muscles. She quickly shook her head clear of the image of him in basketball shorts.

"Sorry, gosh, I guess your love life is a sore subject," Nick joked as he pushed her shoulder.

"Piss off," she said again, only this time there was no steam behind her words.

Nick chuckled. "So, are you going to watch my final ride?"

"Nope," she lied. "I'm going to close my eyes the entire time just to spite you." She sat down in the empty spot her parents had just vacated.

It wasn't the first time they'd left her to fend for herself in the small town. Nor, she doubted, would it be the last. She was old enough and, as they said, Nick had given her plenty of rides home.

Cedar, Wyoming, had a population of about three thousand people, each of which she knew personally. That made it really easy to bum a ride. If she couldn't, it was only six miles back to the ranch, so she could walk.

The only really great thing about Cedar was that it was positioned directly next to Yellowstone National Park.

Which meant that, come summertime, there were a million tourists spending their money in the small town. There was also the added benefit of having all those hot guys flirt with her whenever she was in town.

Nick sat down next to her and continued to talk while she ate her burger. He droned on about his time, his method, even the bulls he was fixing on riding.

"Looks like you're up," she said, motioning to Jimmy, who was frantically waving at Nick.

"Oh, yeah." Nick sprung up. "Wish me luck."

"Break a leg," she said dryly. On the inside, though, her nerves were on edge, and she had to push aside the rest of her burger. Her stomach was tied in a knot watching Nick climb onto the back of another bull, a huge red one with white marks across its nose and between its eyes.

"Next up is Nick Howe..."—the announcer dragged out the 'w' in Nick's last name—"riding McGuire's bull Apollo."

Kara winced. Apollo was known to be the meanest bull in the county. It had even attacked Mr. McGuire last year in the field. Gave him a scar three inches long in his left butt cheek. Or so the rumors said.

Everyone cheered as the buzzer sounded and Nick and the bull jumped out of the gate. Kara held her breath and counted.

She didn't get far, as Nick was thrown clear of the bull's back just two seconds into the ride.

Nick seemed pleased as he got up and dusted himself off. But Apollo had a different plan and headed directly towards Nick.

Kara jumped up and screamed for Nick to run. But Nick just stood there, looking at her. She watched in horror as Apollo's horns headed directly towards Nick. At the last second, Nick seemed to get his wits about him, and he jerked to the side. Only, he wasn't fast enough.

The bull caught Nick in the thigh, and Kara and the rest of the town watched in horror as Nick Howe went flying through the air. Kara couldn't shake the feeling that it was somehow all her fault.

Three years later...

"What do you mean you're not going to leave me in charge?" Kara wanted to stomp her foot. "I'm twenty-one years old. I don't need a babysitter."

Her father smiled down at her. "He's not going to babysit you, just the ranch."

"I've been taking care of the ranch for over thirteen years. I don't need someone to help," she practically yelled.

"Weren't you just complaining last week that we needed to hire more help around here?" Luanna said as she tossed her overnight back over her shoulder.

Kara glared at her. "Someone to help, not to manage," she pointed out.

"Nick won't be managing," her father said. "He's just going to check in on things while we're gone. You know, lend a hand where you need it."

Kara crossed her arms over her chest. "Did you make that clear to him?"

Her father didn't answer. Instead, he picked up their two bags and headed out the door to the waiting car that would take them to the airport. After their luggage was in the trunk, her father turned to her and placed his hands on her shoulders.

"Kare-bear. It's three months. If you need the help, Nick's here. If you don't, I have no doubt you'll send him packing." Her father smiled down at her. "Now, if you need anything—"

"I won't."

Her dad and Luanna had been planning this three-month Eúropean vacation for years. She'd been looking forward to being left in charge for twice as long.

Then her father sprung it on her as they were walking out the door that he'd asked Nick to lend a hand. She knew Nick would translate that as him being left in charge. Like hell.

"Go, have fun." She kissed her father's cheek and then hugged Luanna. "Bring me back something from Paris," she told her stepmother.

"Will do," she replied as she got in the taxi.

Once the car had exited the large wood and iron gates at the end of the drive, she did a quick fist pump and a boogie dance.

She had the entire ranch all to herself for three whole months. Three whole months!

She danced around the large front porch singing. Three whole months to herself.

Oliver, their ten-year-old mutt, watched her little dance from his spot in the corner before losing interest and falling back to sleep.

"Now that's a sight."

The deep voice made her scream and jerk around quickly, and she caught her elbow on the doorjamb of the front door.

Wincing with pain, she glared down at Nick, who was leaning against the railing at the base of the porch stairs. Where had he come from? Had he been standing there the entire time that she'd been making a fool out of herself?

"What do you want?" she asked, her happy and excited mood now sour.

CHAPTER TWO

Irritation crossed Kara's face, a face Nick had memorized so many years ago. A face he dreamed of. A face that he hoped one day would look at him the way he looked at her.

Still, that slight irritation had him smiling. If she was upset at him, at least she was thinking of him. Right?

"I'm here by request of your father," Nick answered. "He wants me to watch the place while he and your stepmother are gone for the next three months," he said, even though he knew it was a stretch.

Carl Montgomery had just asked him to check in on Kara and lend a hand whenever she needed it. But Kara didn't need to know that. The more he was around, the better chance he'd have of finally asking her out.

Kara's eyes ran over him. He could see more annoyance there and smiled even more.

"You're only here to lend a hand *if* I need it." She put a long emphasis on the word *if*.

"That's not what your father told me," he said, moving up the stairs until he could lean against the railing beside her. The porch blocked the sun so he could see Kara's face more clearly.

The face that always had his heart racing and his breathing go jagged. Still, he had learned long ago—since that first day when he'd fallen off Hunter and ended up on his butt in front of her—how to play it cool around her.

From that moment, watching her disappear on her pony, he'd sworn that he would never lose his cool around her again. Over the years he'd tried dating other girls. At several points in his life, he'd convinced himself that he could overcome the crush that he'd had on Kara from the moment he'd spotted her standing by the creek.

Then he'd break off with the temporary distraction and his gaze would fall on Kara again. Always back to Kara.

"I'm here, doing what I've been asked," he corrected. He remembered the long conversation he'd had with her father. What he'd been asked to do.

It wasn't as if Carl didn't trust Kara to run the ranch. He did. Hell, Kara was probably more capable than most of the hired hands they had helping out around his place.

Kara ran her eyes over him, then raised her chin slightly. "If you won't leave, then you can start this morning by mucking out all the stalls." She turned and walked through the screen door, letting it slam loudly behind her. The thing almost came completely off its hinges when it shut.

Since he planned on keeping the promise to her dad to help, he headed towards the barn to check on the animals. Montgomery Ranch wasn't as large as Howe Ranch, but still, there were enough animals in the barn that it took him almost two hours to muck out all the stalls and check on the animals. He made sure to give them each personal time.

They had four horses, three goats that roamed the property in a huge pen, and a rather angry looking pig called Wilbur. When Nick tried to check on him, Wilbur had chased him out of his pen. There were also chickens that were put into a portable cage that every day moved a few feet to new grazing areas. That was in addition to the hundred or so head of cattle.

Howe Ranch had easily twice that in cattle. Besides his two border collies, Lenny and Squiggy, there were goats, chickens, and at least a half a dozen friendly pigs. He also had more than a dozen horses in various stages of being broken and trained. That was his sole job on the ranch. Most of the horses they didn't own themselves. They had been dropped off by their owners for him to work with.

It usually took him a few months to break a horse and tame them. But he did more than mere rein and saddle work, so he normally had the horses for eight months or more, depending on what level of training the owners wanted.

He'd come up with the business idea after his short career as a bull rider had ended. Abruptly. Being in the hospital for two months with broken bones and ruptured organs had caused him to reevaluate his future. He supposed it had been bound to happen sooner or later. He'd just wished he'd had a few medals and enough money under his belt to build the future he'd dreamed of—a nice log cabin somewhere on acreage of his own with a wife, a couple kids, and some dogs.

It didn't scare him when he thought of all that. Instantly, images of brown-haired blue-eyed kids came to mind. Hell, he really did have to start wooing Kara. The least he could do was not annoy her so much in the next three months.

"What are you doing?" Kara's voice shook him out of his thoughts.

He turned to see her standing with her hands on her hips, glaring at him. She had on her riding outfit, and her dark hair was pulled back in braids, instantly reminding him of the day they'd met by the stream.

"Feeding and watering the pig," he answered easily as he turned back to the task.

Kara walked over and grabbed the water hose that he'd been using to fill the trough. When she turned it off, he frowned.

"I was just—" he started, but she held up a hand to stop him.

"I said you could muck out the stalls. You should have left after that." She took a deep breath. "I'll handle the rest."

"Afraid of a little help?" He leaned against the low fence and smiled.

"I'm not afraid of anything," she ground out slowly. "Now, I'm heading out for a ride. You can go."

"Go?" he asked, faking ignorance.

"Leave. Go home." Kara waved her hands in the direction of his property.

He thought for a moment and then smiled. "How about I help you exercise Larry?" He nodded to the older horse who was standing next to her horse, Bella.

"Larry is fine," Kara said. She set down the hose and walked towards Bella, who eagerly nudged Kara's shoulder, no doubt excited for the upcoming ride. Larry stood there, looking sad and pathetic and uninterested.

"Larry needs love too," he said, falling in step with Kara.

Kara glared over at him. "Larry is too old."

"I wouldn't say that. He's just... seasoned." He felt sad for the beast. He remembered the day they'd gotten him.

He'd been young. Energetic. One of the most beautiful horses he'd seen up to that point. He still was. His smooth white coat practically shined in the sunlight. He walked over and ran his hands over the horse's mane and leaned into the horse to whisper how handsome he was.

When he realized it had grown quiet, he glanced over to see Kara watching him with a strange look on her face. Their eyes locked and for the first time in a while, he could have sworn he saw heat in those blue eyes. As quickly as it had appeared, it was gone, replaced with the annoyance she always had when dealing with him.

"Larry is not going on today's ride," Kara said a little more firmly.

Nick ignored Kara and walked over and grabbed one of their saddles and started carting it over to put on Larry.

Kara followed him and continued to try and persuade him that it wasn't a good idea. After she realized that he wasn't going to back down, she started saddling Bella. He thought for a moment that she'd call the ride off, but then he remembered that she was too stubborn. She lived for challenges.

No doubt she'd try to race him. But he respected Larry too much to push the old horse. Sometimes, slow and steady wins the race in different ways.

He smiled as he watched her jump onto Bella's back. He'd already climbed into the saddle and was waiting at the corral gate.

"Ready?" he asked.

As her answer, Kara's chin rose slightly, and she tipped her hat down to shade her eyes.

"I'll take that as a yes," he joked as Bella and Kara stepped through the gate. He maneuvered Larry through and then shut it behind them.

They set off across the field, heading in the opposite direction from his place. The Montgomery's land may have been much smaller than his, but they still had more than a hundred acres.

"Where are we off to?" he asked, keeping Larry in step with Bella.

"I," Kara said, dragging out the word, "am checking the east fence."

He smiled. "Okay, you check out the fence. I'll just let old Larry here stretch his legs." He patted Larry on the neck, earning him a snort from the older horse.

"He doesn't like to be called old," Kara retorted.

"He can understand?" Nick joked.

"He's old, of course he can," Kara said, causing Larry to snort again. "Sorry, Larry," Kara added quickly, causing Nick to smile.

"Okay, I'll let Larry here stretch his legs then." He gave Larry another pat. This time the horse nodded his head as if he agreed. Damn, the horse was really that smart. He'd trained plenty of horses over the past few years, but none had even come close to understanding him. Well, except Crash. He and Crash had an understanding that the horse was fully in charge. One hundred percent of the time.

Nick was smiling when Kara asked, "Don't you have a ranch of your own to see after?"

"Sure, and plenty of hired hands to help out," he answered smoothly. "I made a promise to your pa that I'd lend a hand, so here I am." He shifted slightly in the saddle. "Why? Don't you like having company?"

Kara narrowed her eyes at him. "I can take care of my ranch on my own."

"I don't doubt that." He relaxed in the saddle. "While most girls your age are busy trying to decide what shoes go with their purses, you're out here feeding and watering pigs." He'd meant it as a compliment, but the look on her face had him wishing he'd kept his mouth shut. "I only meant—" he started, but she held up her hand.

"I get it. Still, that was a very sexist remark," she said dryly before kicking Bella into a trot. He instantly felt bad about what he'd said and wanted to catch up with her but didn't want to push Larry. Instead, he followed her to the fence line and silently cursed his words.

The next time he was close to her, he was helping her repair some barbed wire fence. They didn't talk. Didn't even really look at one another. It was going to be a very long three months.

As he headed back to his place for lunch an hour later, he cursed himself for not being as smooth as he was with other girls. Hell, he'd had six girlfriends since he'd started dating. Six. Most of all of them he was still pretty friendly with.

Nick saw his dad sitting in the swing on the front porch of the main house with the dogs lying at his feet and headed that way instead of the small cabin he'd been living in at the back of the property. He'd moved into it and had fixed it up shortly after his eighteenth birthday, once he'd healed from his injuries.

At one point in his life, he'd planned on moving away, out of state. Then he'd been injured and, well, after that, his father's health had started going downhill.

His parents had Nick late in life. His mother had been forty-two. His father fifty-six. He was their miracle child, the one they had never planned on having but thanked god for every day of their lives. They had tried for so many years before and after his birth, but he was their only joy.

His mother had died shortly after his thirteenth

birthday of breast cancer. His father was currently struggling with his second bout of cancer himself. His was somewhat self-inflicted from all the years he'd smoked. Even now, as Nick stepped onto the porch, he could smell the hint of the cigarette his father had tried to hide from him.

"Dad," he said, his voice the only warning his father needed to understand that he hadn't fooled him.

"It was just one," his father said, then he coughed several times.

"That's all it takes," Nick said, sitting beside his father. Over the past few years, his dad had grown frail. He was no longer the boisterous strong man that had taught Nick how to bust broncos or rope steer. Instead, the man who sat beside him seemed well past his expiration date. That ate at Nick.

"Helping out over at the Montgomery place?" his father said, changing the subject.

"Yes," Nick said, sending the swing rocking slowly. His eyes zoned across the land to the dot in the distance that was Kara's home.

"That girl..." his father started.

"Kara," Nick supplied, knowing full well his father knew her name.

"Yeah. She sure is a pretty young thing and smart to boot." His father gave him a side glance. "You ever going to make your move on her?"

Nick narrowed his eyes. "How long was it before you made your moves on Ma?" Nick asked.

His father chuckled, then coughed. "Too damn long. But I raised you to be smarter than me." His dad slapped him on the shoulder as he stood up. "Don't be an idiot like I was and waste half your life building up the courage to ask the woman out." His father glanced out over the field. "You never know how long you got."

His father walked inside, leaving him sitting on the porch with the dogs, wishing he really was smarter than his old man.

CHAPTER THREE

The following day, Kara woke with a start when she heard pounding outside. She lay there for a moment thinking she'd dreamed the noise, then she heard a drill and jumped out of bed.

Without thinking, she rushed to the front door and yanked it open to see Nick kneeling inside the doorway. He was holding a drill in his hands and had several long screws held between his lips.

When she yanked open the door, his eyes flew to hers.

"What in the hell are you doing?" she asked, angrily.

She watched his eyes move away from hers to slide down her body. It was then that she realized what she was wearing. Realized that she hadn't grabbed her robe.

Her bright red and white candy-striped pajamas with the massive reindeer head in the middle of her chest had been a Christmas gift the year before. They were her most comfortable pajamas, and she normally wore them on chilly nights. She also wore them on nights she struggled with menstrual pain, as was the case last night.

When Nick's eyes returned to hers, he smiled and

removed the screws from his mouth. "Christmas is still over two months away," he pointed out.

"What are you doing?" she asked, gritting her teeth.

His smile slipped a little. "Fixing your screen door. When you slammed it in my face yesterday, it almost came off its hinges." He got back to work.

She wanted to argue with him, but she had noticed it and had added it to her own to-do list. She watched him putting in a few long screws and realized she wouldn't have thought to replace the screws with longer ones. Over the years, she'd just tightened the ones that was there, which meant she had to do it more and more often.

Not wanting to argue with the man, she slammed the front door and headed in so that she could shower and dress. She didn't want Nick to get any more of a head start on her. After all, this was supposed to be her time to show her parents that she was capable of running the place on her own.

If Nick did everything, she was sure he would pass that bit of information along to her father when he returned.

After showering, she pulled on a pair of comfortable jeans and put a warm flannel shirt over her tank top. Wiping the steam from her mirror, she frowned at her reflection.

It had stung what Nick had said yesterday. She'd hated that it had. How many times had she wished she could be something different. A girlie girl. One that liked to wear pink. Liked dresses. Knew how to do her hair and makeup like all those videos she watched at night. But whenever she tried, she just looked... strange and ended up wiping it all off.

It wasn't as if she was a total tomboy. She did like wearing earrings, necklaces, and the little blue ring her mother had given her long before she'd died. She even liked the thought of wearing dresses. When summer came around, she'd pull out her sundresses for church or special occasions. She loved summer.

But to work around the property, she normally wore worn jeans, T-shirts (or flannels during colder days), and work boots. Her long straight dark hair was nothing special. Its color reminded her of mud. Just plain old mud. One year she'd convinced her dad to allow her to get highlights. She'd ended up hating them after everyone had made fun of her.

She pulled her hair back into a ponytail and took a moment to put on a little eyeliner and mascara. If she did anything more, Nick would assume she was doing it for him.

Deep down in her heart, she knew she sort of was. She hated that thought, as it was obvious that he didn't think of her in that way. All his ex-girlfriends had been the cheerleader type. Two were even past beauty queens. One had been the town's Miss Christmas in the previous year's parade.

Nick, along with every other guy in town her age, went after the girlie girls, not the tomboy type that she was.

Stepping into the kitchen, she almost screamed when Nick held up a mug of coffee.

"What are you doing in here?" she asked.

"Coffee?" he said, ignoring her question.

Since she needed the boost and it was already made, she took the mug.

"You didn't lock the door." He turned to make another cup for himself.

"That's not an invitation for you to just waltz in and make coffee." She took a sip of the coffee, swallowing the moan of pleasure. After three sips, she set the mug down and walked over to the freezer to pull out some frozen waffles.

"That's not breakfast," Nick said, shaking his head.

"It's what I'm having," she said, popping two waffles into the toaster.

"You've got to have something better than that." Nick walked to the fridge and bent over, looking inside.

Her eyes instantly went to his ass. He was wearing jeans just as worn as hers, only his fit… exceptionally well. The man had an ass that made her mouth water.

She didn't realize he was still talking until he glanced back and looked at her, his eyebrows rising slightly.

"What?" she asked, shaking her head to clear thoughts of his ass.

"You have fresh eggs in here and bacon," he repeated.

"And no time to make them," she said as her waffles popped up.

Nick took the hot waffles and gave them to Oliver, who gobbled them up so quickly, she couldn't help but smile.

"Hey." She tried to reach around him, but he laughed.

"It takes three minutes to cook eggs." He wrapped his hands around her wrists. "Five for bacon."

"So." She jerked her arm free. "I'm hungry now."

"Sit." He smiled and pointed to the table. "I'll cook. Drink your coffee. You're feisty this morning."

She narrowed her eyes and might have told him to fuck off under her breath as she sat down.

Since she'd been woken abruptly from a really good dream, she closed her eyes and took several more drinks of her coffee to calm herself down.

When she opened her eyes again, Nick was standing at her stove, flipping bacon and eggs as if he was an expert line cook.

"Why?" she asked between sips, "are you being a thorn in my side?"

He glanced over his shoulder and smiled at her, and she felt her heart kick in her chest. Damn, he was cute. Too cute. Her heart slipped again, and her stomach dropped when she realized she couldn't have him. Would never have him.

She looked down into her coffee and thought about her future once more. She'd been on the edge of leaving town. Heading into the city for college. Maybe Denver? But as usual, she didn't know what she'd go to school for. She loved what she did here. Loved being a rancher. Loved working with the animals every day.

"Why the long face?" Nick asked as he set a plate of eggs and bacon in front of her. There were two slices of buttered toast on the side as well, and he'd set a huge dollop of homemade raspberry jelly that she'd bought at the last farmer's market on them.

When he placed a plate down across from hers and sat down, he glanced up at her. "See, isn't this much better?"

"Do you plan on eating here every morning?" she asked, dryly.

He smiled. "Maybe. Are you always this cheerful in the morning?"

She grunted as she took a bite of the eggs and then frowned. They were good. Really good. Better than any she'd made before. Taking another bite, she confirmed it. They were the best eggs she'd ever had.

"What did you do to these eggs?" she asked.

Nick smiled. "A chef doesn't reveal his secrets."

"That code is only for magicians," she said dryly.

He chuckled. "And chefs."

"You're not a chef." She took another bite.

"I'm glad you like them," he said, taking a bite of his own eggs.

By the time she was done with the eggs, she was pretty sure his secret ingredients were cheese, butter, and salt. Either way, she didn't want him to get too big of a head about it, so she kept her mouth shut for the rest of the meal.

When he was finished eating, he took his plate to the sink, rinsed it, and stuck it in the dishwasher. At that very moment, she fell in love with Nick Howe.

Damn it.

"Finished?" he asked her. When she nodded, he repeated the process with her plate.

"Why are you being so kind today? Yesterday you were..." She paused and then added, "Not so kind."

He chuckled and leaned against the counter, his eyes running slowly over her like they always did.

"I think we got off on the wrong foot. If we're going to be working with each other for the next couple of months—"

"We won't. You're not needed."

His smile increased. "We've established I'll be here whether you want me or not, so I figured we might as well be cordial to one another."

She sighed heavily and finished off her second cup of coffee.

"Feel better?" he asked, watching her.

"Better?" She frowned.

His eyebrows shot up. "You were... Not so kind earlier," he said, throwing her words back at her.

She bit the inside of her lip, trying to stop the flood of words from spilling from her mouth. Standing up, she slowly exhaled and released everything she wanted to say, then put her coffee mug in the dishwasher and walked out without saying a word.

The next time she saw him, he was talking to the pig. Wilbur didn't like anyone. Ever. Yet, Nick was standing just inside the fence, leaning on it as if he was very comfortable, talking to the pig, who was just looking at him.

"What are you doing?" she asked, moving slowly towards the pig pen.

Nick glanced over his shoulder. "Just having a discussion with Wilbur. We've come to an agreement. Haven't we?" Nick asked the pig, who just stared back at him.

"An... agreement?" She wanted to pull Nick over the fence before the pig could attack him.

"Sure." Nick chuckled. "I'll feed him my famous gruel each day if he promises not to kill me."

She frowned and watched Wilbur lose interest in them and go back to eating the mixture in his trough.

"Why are you so determined to be friends with Wilbur?" she asked, leaning against the fence.

"Why hasn't anyone tried to get him to be friendly?" he countered.

"Because he's Christmas dinner," she said with a shrug.

"What?" Nick gasped and shook his head. "You don't eat family." He turned back to Wilbur.

She chuckled. "He's not family. My dad buys a new pig each year just for Christmas."

"No." Nick frowned. "You've had Wilbur for as long as I can remember."

"Correction, we've had a pig named Wilbur for as long as you can remember," she said easily.

Nick frowned at that and looked back at the pig. "You call different pigs by the same name?"

"My father claims it keep him from getting too attached

to his food." Kara shrugged again and glanced off over the field. She felt a little steadier after the bigger meal, but she wasn't about to let Nick know that.

Nick jumped out of the pen and shoved his hands into his jean pockets. "Gosh, that just... that's not right." He shook his head as his eyes returned to Wilbur.

Kara could have sworn she saw sadness flash behind his eyes, but then he shifted, and the sun blocked her view of his face.

"Didn't you just make me bacon this morning?" she laughed.

"Yeah, but..." He shook his head and then glanced away. "Is that why you have two turkeys?"

"Gobble and Giblets." She smiled. "Normally, they'd be Thanksgiving and Christmas, but since my parents won't be back until after the New Year, one of them will be spared until Easter. I've was thinking of supplying the turkey and pig since Liz's family has offered to let me crash their Thanksgiving and Christmas dinners."

When he made another loud sigh, she turned so she could see his face more clearly. She couldn't understand why he was making a big deal about it. After all, he had more cattle, chickens, and pigs than they did. "You eat your cattle, right?"

"Yes," he said quickly. "When I'm in charge, I want to change things up."

"Are you going vegetarian on me?"

"No." He frowned. "Just... a little more... humane."

"I think we're as humane as we can be. We keep the animals happy and fed. We allow them to graze." She waved her arms around the land.

"Right, it's just..." he looked back to Wilbur. "Why name him Wilbur? They didn't slaughter him in the book."

"It was my father's idea." She straightened and stretched. The large breakfast had her feeling lethargic. Normally, she didn't eat as much before all her chores were done.

Nick seemed to realize that the conversation had changed and glanced around the paddock.

"What else can I help out with today?" he asked.

She thought about the list of items that she'd been putting off—chores she dreaded or outright hated—and smiled.

CHAPTER FOUR

Nick cursed as a large clump of black grease fell in his face for the second time. Was it even really one of her chores to grease the bearings on the old tractor that appeared to have not even been turned on in the past year?

To get to the right spot, he'd had to army crawl over the mucky floor in the old barn. He wiped the grease from his face and smeared it back into the tube that he shoved into the wheel axle joint. If he hadn't spent a few years working on this tractor himself, he wouldn't have known just how to push the grease into the hidden spots. But a few years back, his dad had sold Mr. Montgomery this old thing, so Nick knew all there was to know about how to maintain it.

When a pair of cowboy boots appeared next to his head, he glanced up.

"Is that you, Nick?" Liz Wilson asked as she knelt down to smile at him. Liz was Kara's best friend.

He'd always thought that the tanned, carefree, bleached blonde would have blended in better on a beach somewhere holding a surfboard rather than wearing horse riding gear.

"Hey, Liz," he said easily and scooted the rest of the way out from under the tractor.

"What in the heck are you doing to this old thing?" Liz asked, kicking the tire with her boot.

"Greasing it." He wiped his hands on the rag he'd used to wipe his face.

Liz laughed. "I can see that." She took the rag from him and wiped his chin. "There," she said just as someone cleared their throat.

They both looked over to the barn door, where Kara was standing with her hands on her hips. "There you are, Liz. I saw your jeep out front." Kara glared at Nick for a moment. "Ready for our ride?" she asked her friend.

"Sure." Liz smiled at him as she handed him back the rag. "It's a good thing Kara has you around helping out." Liz patted his shoulder.

"Right," he said as the two friends left the barn.

His days started to bleed into one another. By the ended of the third week of helping out around Kara's ranch, he was beginning to believe she was just having him do the shit jobs no one around the place wanted to touch. Still, he enjoyed seeing her and spending time with her so much that he didn't mind.

As with each day, he headed back to his property shortly before lunchtime to catch up on his own tasks for the day. Every evening, by the time he'd showered off the dust and dirt from the day, he was sore, tired, and, oddly, horny as hell.

Thanksgiving came and went. He enjoyed cooking a big meal for his dad and some of the employees who couldn't be with their families. It was a tradition his mother had started, and he continued each holiday.

He was happy when he noticed that both of her turkeys

were still in their paddocks after the holiday. He wondered if she had changed her mind about her Christmas meal as well.

He had taken a day to decorate the house, hoping it would lift his and his father's spirits and keep his dad happy even as his health grew worse.

He also helped Kara decorate her place, even though she'd told him she didn't plan to do it since her folks wouldn't be back by the holiday.

Still, he'd convinced her, and they had spent an entire day hanging festive lights around her place and setting up a tree that he'd chopped down for her when he'd picked out his own tree on their property.

Her irritation about him being around disappeared for the most part. Every now and then, it would surface, but he'd work through it and, with the power of flirting, he'd get her to relax.

But with each day he spent with Kara, the more dangerous flirting with her became. He knew that soon he wouldn't be able to keep his feelings to himself. Soon, he'd have to kiss her. Soon, he'd have to show her what he felt for her.

It had been almost six months since he'd been out on a date. Even longer since he'd had sex.

He'd been helping Kara out for almost two months now. Each day, he'd helped her and held his feelings for her back. He knew it was only a matter of time before she did or said something that would cause him to lose control of his desire for her and do what he'd wanted to do for a long time —kiss her.

Deciding to let the cool evening air clear his mind, he stepped outside to see his dad collapsed on the porch.

He dialed 911 as he rushed over to check his father for a

pulse. Feeling a faint one, he relayed the information to the operator and held his father until the ambulance showed up.

When they pulled away, he climbed into his truck to follow them to the hospital. As he pulled out, Kara was standing at the end of her drive, looking worried, so he pulled over.

"What's wrong?" she asked, hugging her jacket closer to her.

"My father." He shook his head.

"Is he?" she asked, a worried look in her eyes.

"He's alive. I'm not sure how long he was unconscious," he admitted.

"Want me to come along?" she asked him. At that moment, he felt his worry slip a little.

"No, thanks. We may be at the hospital all night."

"I can check on your animals in the morning?" she offered.

He shook his head again. "Thanks, we've got Daryl to do all that."

"Keep me posted. I won't keep you." She motioned to the road.

He started to roll up his window. "Thanks for the offer," he said, and then he drove away.

By the time they moved his father to a private room, the doctors had already talked to him. His father's cancer had progressed. Last time they'd given his father years. This time, it was months, weeks, or even days.

He felt like punching something. Instead, he sat in the chair next to his father's bed and held his hand and tried to think of what life was going to be like without the old man.

Most of his friends from school had always complained

about their fathers. How they couldn't wait to get away from them after school.

Nick had never felt like that about his dad. Never. His father was the man who had shown him how to do... well, everything. Before Nick had made friends in school, he'd had his dad.

Nicholas Howe the second was and always would be Nick's best friend. He couldn't remember a time when Nick hadn't looked up to the man.

Now, as he glanced down at his and his father's hands, he wondered just when the man had gotten frail. Nick remembered these hands teaching him how to tie a rope. How to haul in a steer. How to tighten a bolt on a car or a piece of machinery they were working on. How to hammer in a nail.

A tear rolled down his nose and landed on their joined hands.

"What's all this?" His father's shaky voice broke him from his thoughts.

"You're awake," Nick said, sitting up and wiping his face with his free hand.

"Sure am. You're soaking me, son." His father motioned to their hands.

"Sorry, sir." Nick smiled. "You gave me a scare."

"Sorry, son." His father smiled. "I just couldn't catch my breath." He shook his head. "Damn," he said after looking around. "I'm back here? I hate the food here."

Nick chuckled. "If you're good, I'll bring you a burger tomorrow."

"Tomorrow? Why can't they let me go now? I'm awake, ain't I?" His father tried to sit up.

Nick jumped up and hit the button on the bed, making it sit up for him.

"I can do it." His father waved his hand and took over hitting the button. "Damn, I keep meaning to get one of these at home so I can sit up and do my crossword puzzles in bed."

Nick smiled. His father was always doing puzzles or reading the paper. Not many people still ordered the paper in town. His father always joked that he was single-handedly responsible for keeping the local newspaper in business.

"How are you feeling now?" Nick asked, adjusting the oxygen tube strapped to his father's face.

"Fine, fine," his father said, shifting slightly. "Well, what's the doc say this time?"

Nick's face fell. His eyes moved back to his father's hands.

"That bad, huh?" His father sighed. "Well, I knew it was coming," his father said after a moment. "Guess it's time I put my foot down."

"On?" Nick asked, his eyes going to his dad's.

"I promised your ma that I wouldn't leave this place until you'd found yourself someone to share it with," his father shocked him by saying. "I had hoped you'd get around to the task on your own." His father winked.

"What are you talking about?" He frowned again.

"Marriage, boy. I'm talking about you settling down with someone." His father chuckled, then went into a coughing spree.

"Dad." Nick shook his head and sat back down after his father stopped coughing. "You should get some rest."

"Soon I'll be getting plenty of that. Now it's time I did what I should have done a while back."

"What's that?" Nick asked, worried that his father wasn't making any sense.

"Give you an ultimatum." His father nodded his head once. "That's what you need."

"Me?" Nick frowned.

"Let's see, I think by Christmas. That should give you enough time." His father smiled.

"For what?" Nick was thinking about ringing for the nurse.

"To find yourself a wife." His father relaxed back. "Or I'll sell the ranch to Wilbert. He's been hounding me for years about it." He shut his eyes.

"What?" Nick said loudly, but his father had either fallen asleep or was faking it to avoid arguing.

Nick spent the night in the hospital chair next to his father's bed, waking each time a nurse came in to check on his father. By morning, his back hurt and he was growing more worried about his father.

A quarter after eight, there was a light knock on the door.

"Come in," he called out, standing up and stretching. His father was awake already, doing a puzzle from the local paper he'd requested.

Kara walked in holding a large bundle of flowers. "Morning," she said cheerfully. "Beth out there tells me you're doing great," she said to his father.

"Well, there she is." His father set down the paper and smiled up at Kara. "Flowers? For me?" He chuckled softly.

Nick noticed that his father held in a cough this time. "Wow, it's been years since anyone's gotten me flowers." He winked at Kara as she set them down on a table next to his bed.

"How are you feeling this morning?" Kara asked as her eyes ran over his father.

"Much better now that they hooked me up to some fresh air," he joked, motioning to his oxygen tube.

"Well, I remembered how much you hated the food here, so..." She pulled out a small Tupperware container from her bag and set it in front of her father. "Don't tell the nurses," Kara said with a wink.

His father opened the lid to a large slice of coffee cake. His father loved coffee cake.

"I made it fresh this morning," Kara said, handing him a fork.

"Do I get a slice?" he asked, feeling his stomach growl.

Kara frowned. "I... wasn't sure if you'd still be here."

"Why don't you do me a favor," his father broke in, then took a bite and groaned. "Damn good cake," he added. "Take this kid of mine off my hands for a while. His hovering is bothering me." His father waved his hand. "Maybe the two of you could head down to the diner and grab some breakfast." He took another bite. "I have a feeling after all this sugar, I'm going to need a nap."

"Dad," Nick started, but his father narrowed his eyes at him, and he shut his mouth.

"I'm sure Kara hasn't had time to eat anything herself, with all the baking she did for me this morning."

"I..." Kara started, but his father narrowed his eyes in her direction, and she chuckled. "I could eat," she finished.

"Good. Now go and leave an old man to enjoy this treat alone." His father waved them away.

He turned to Kara and frowned. "You don't have to..." he started, but she waved him off after raising her chin slightly.

"Come on, the diner is just across the street." Kara walked back out without waiting for him. He followed her into the elevator and, as the doors slid closed, she turned to him and asked. "So, how's he really doing?"

Leaning against the wall, he sighed.

"That bad?" she asked. He nodded. "The cancer is back?"

"It never left," he answered. "Just... grew. The doc says he's got days or weeks instead of years."

Kara laid a hand on his arm. He hadn't realized just how hard it was hitting him until he felt her hand on his skin.

Through the haze of telling himself not to break down in front of her, he heard the elevator doors open. She tugged on his arm, and he followed her out of the hospital and across the street like a zombie.

They were seated in a corner booth, and he sat in silence as Kara ordered them both coffees. He sipped the hot drink, then frowned and put in creamer and sugar.

"Are you okay?" she asked him after he took a sip.

"Yeah," he sighed, remembering what his father had told him about selling the ranch. His eyes zoned in on the dark liquid. "Did you always plan on staying at your folks' place?"

Kara was quiet for a moment. "No, not always. When I was ten, I thought I'd run away and join the circus. I was going to be one of the ladies that rode on the horses' backs in tights with a large feather in my hair." She smiled and he smiled with her.

"I could totally see that." He felt his heart lighten. "The way you used to ride that pony of yours." He laughed as he remembered seeing her standing on the little horse's back plenty of times. "You were getting pretty good at it."

She was smiling at him. "What about you?"

His smile slipped. "Not always." He looked up at her.

"That bull made my decision for me." He rubbed his left thigh, which still pained him when it got too cold. The scar wasn't as bad as it had once been. Most of the damage had been internal. The scars were there just to remind him of what could have been. The misstep that he'd almost taken.

CHAPTER FIVE

Kara felt a wave of guilt wash over her as she watched Nick's eyes change while he talked about how he had planned on following the rodeo circuit after school.

His injury that day was her fault, and she avoided his gaze as he continued. But then his story shifted, and he talked about his family's ranch as if it was the best place on the planet. He went on about his plans for the place. How he wanted to turn part of it into a rehabilitation center for abused animals and wayward teens.

The more he talked about his idea over breakfast, the more light came into his eyes and, if she was honest with herself, the more she was drawn into his plans.

"So, what does your dad think of your plans?" she asked after their table was cleared of the empty dishes.

Nick frowned for the first time since he's started sharing his ideas.

"I... haven't talked to him about it yet," he admitted.

She thought about how fragile his dad had looked, how vulnerable, and wondered if Nick had kept his thoughts to himself out of fear of his father's health.

"It's not..." he started, then shook his head. "How about a walk?" he asked, nodding towards the windows.

When she'd woken that morning, it had been raining. Now, however, there was a break in the clouds and the sun was shining. Even though it was still a crisp winter morning in Wyoming, it was nice out.

"Sure." She pulled out her purse and tried to pay for her half of breakfast, but Nick stopped her and paid the entire bill.

"It's the least I can do after you baked for my dad."

They strolled out of the diner and headed towards the center of town. There was a park right in front of the city building. Normally, on spring and summer days, kids and families filled the space. Now, however, it was empty. Holiday decorations adorned every light post and tree in the area. The gazebo in the center of the park area was completely decked out. A massive Christmas tree sat directly across the gazebo and had been officially lit the day after Thanksgiving, as was the town's tradition.

They walked around the pathway and sat on a bench facing the huge tree.

How many times had she and her family enjoyed the park together? There had been summer concerts, movie nights, fall and winter festivals, not to mention her high school graduation party, which had been held around the gazebo area just across the grass under a million hanging string lights.

"This place is home." He sighed and leaned back.

"I was thinking the same thing." She smiled at him.

"I had my first kiss..." He motioned to a large tree known to the townspeople as the kissing tree.

"Seriously? You did the whole kissing tree thing?" She nudged his shoulder with her own.

"How do you think it got its name?" He smiled at her, and she realized that his smile was slightly crooked, which made her heart do a little flip. "I managed to get Leslie Thomas to sneak away from the summer festival and kiss me until her brother came looking for her." He chuckled. "I earned a black eye for that move. What about you?"

She shook her head. "I've never kissed under the tree."

"Where was your first kiss?"

"Under the bleachers," she admitted. "Shelby Logan." She smiled. "Before he and his family moved to California."

He narrowed his eyes, as if trying to remember the boy. "He played basketball?"

"Football," she corrected.

"Right." He sighed and looked out over the park. "I can't believe my dad only has days left. Maybe a couple weeks."

She held her breath, knowing the sorrow he must be feeling, and then took his hand in hers, unsure how to help him through the pain.

He looked down at their hands. "I should get back..." he said but didn't move.

"Nick, you don't need to spread yourself thin. I can run my ranch fine while my folks are gone," she said, unsure of why she thought it was important to say.

His eyes moved up to hers. "I like helping out. It keeps my mind off..." He closed his eyes, and she was afraid that she would see a tear slip down his cheek. Instead, he looked at their joined hands again. "I like helping."

She didn't want to take something away from him that was helping him through a dark time, so she nodded.

"Okay." She shifted a little when the wind kicked up.

"You're cold." He stood up and pulled her with him. "Let's head back."

She wanted to tell him she was fine, but the truth was, the warm sunlight had been blocked by clouds and the temperature had dropped several degrees.

"We're supposed to get snow later this week," he said as they walked.

"When are they going to release your dad?" she asked.

"In a few hours. After the doctor..." He dropped off. "My dad signed a DNR this morning."

She frowned. "DNR?"

"Do not resuscitate. It's a legal form that tells everyone that he's ready to go," he said, his voice low.

She felt her heart break a little more. "I'm so sorry," she said, remembering her own mother's death. She'd been so young that most of what her mother had gone through had been kept from her. Even now, she didn't understand exactly what her parents had gone through during that difficult time.

"After my mother went, Dad made all the arrangements for himself." He stopped just outside the hospital doors. "I can't imagine making plans like that."

She wanted to say something to him. To comfort him further, but just then the doors opened, and a young couple came out, walking past them into the parking lot.

"I'll let you get home. Thanks again for stopping by." He dropped her hand finally.

"Nick?" she said when he turned to walk inside. He stopped and looked over his shoulder at her. "If you need anything, I'm here." He nodded and disappeared inside.

Since she'd made the trip into town, she figured she'd head over and visit Liz at work. Her best friend owned one of the three beauty salons in town. Liz had gone through a yearlong course to get her cosmetology license after graduating from high school. Since her parents owned most of the buildings in town, she'd taken over a vacant building that faced the town square. Get Buzzed was by far the most popular salon in town and the result of her best friend's hard work.

Over the last year, Liz had added several tanning beds, nail stations, and even two private rooms in the back for waxing and massages.

When Kara walked in the door, Liz smiled at her and motioned to the wine bar.

"Grab a mimosa," her friend said as she continued putting foils in Mrs. Sabastian's hair. The old woman was sipping her own mimosa.

Kara grabbed an already mixed drink from the chilled container and then sat down in the empty salon chair next to the one Liz was working at.

"Why the long face?" Liz asked after glancing at her.

"Nick's dad is in the hospital," she answered, taking a sip of the drink.

Mrs. Sabastian and Liz both stopped and glanced at her.

"The cancer's back?" Mrs. Sabastian asked.

"It never went away," Liz answered. "Nick says the doctors have given him days. Weeks if he's lucky."

"Oh no," Mrs. Sabastian said with a slight shake of her head. "I'll have to spread the word."

Mrs. Sabastian and Nick's mother had been friends. Hell, most everyone in town knew one another and was friendly with the exception of a handful of outliers who lived on the outskirts of the town and kept to themselves.

"How's Nick taking it?" Liz asked, getting back to work on Mrs. Sabastian's hair.

"Not so good. I mean, it's obvious he knew this day was coming, but..." She sighed and took another drink. "He'll be all alone." She thought of losing her dad. Her stepmother. She'd always have her half-brother, Beau. But he lived in Hawaii with his new wife, Nicky.

What would happen to the ranch? Had her parents accounted for her desire to take it over? Maybe this time was the test to see if she was capable or worthy.

"Wilbert Howe mentioned the last time Nicholas was in the hospital that he'd come up with a scheme to ensure that Nick wouldn't be alone after his death," Mrs. Sabastian said, gaining their attention.

Liz's hand hung in the air, and a glop of bleach fell to the floor unnoticed. "Well?" Liz said when Mrs. Sabastian didn't continue. "What plan?"

Mrs. Sabastian smiled, enjoying the attention. "Wilbert and Marge have been trying for years to get their hands on the ranch. Everyone knows they believe they should have inherited it after Nicholas the first, Nicholas and Wilbert's father, passed. Well, Wilbert let it drop at the Fourth of July celebration that their son, Willy, should be the rightful heir. So, Wilbert put in motion his plan."

"Which is?" Kara asked, leaning forward slightly.

Willy Howe was Nick's cousin, she thought. Willy's dad, Wilbert, was Nick's dad's younger brother by at least twenty years. The story went that after Nicholas the first's wife had died, Nicholas the first married Wilbert's mother, Carolynn. When Nicholas the first died a few years later, the ranch was left to Nicholas the second, leaving Carolynn and her son, Wilbert, out in the cold. Well, not literally. They ended up moving back into town with Carolynn's brother.

For as long as the town could remember, Wilbert Howe

and his family had been up in arms about getting their hands on the ranch.

"Well," Mrs. Sabastian continued, "it seems Nicholas isn't too pleased that his son hasn't found himself a wife and started a family of his own yet."

Hearing this, Kara's stomach dropped. "And?" she said, not liking the sound of her own low tone.

Mrs. Sabastian leaned closer to her. "And Wilbert let it slip that he'd convinced his brother Nicholas the second to push his boy into marriage by writing it into his will that if the boy wasn't married before the end of the year after his death, the ranch would default to Wilbert and his son, Willy." Mrs. Sabastian smirked. "Like those two would ever deserve what Nicholas and Nicky have worked hard all their lives for." She made a tsking sound as she shook her head.

Kara swallowed and glanced out the windows. "Does Nick know about this?"

"I would think not," Mrs. Sabastian said. "I'm not even sure Nicholas really did change his will. Not for sure. You know how Wilbert and Willy can be."

Willy, or Wil as he demanded to be called, had been the star player in both football and baseball. At one point, he'd asked her out on a date, and she would have said yes if Liz hadn't warned her about a rumor going around that he and his buddies had a bet on who could have sex with her first.

That year, she hadn't dated anyone. Even though he and his friends continued to ask her out.

After that, she'd started seeing through Willy's facade. He was a jerk to anyone weaker or smarter than he was. He was rude to the point of crudeness towards women. Most importantly, he was such a jerk to Nick that it infuriated her.

Was this what Nick was upset about? Was he worried that all his dreams would disappear just because he wasn't married? Was that why he was so interested in her place? She stiffened at that thought. Then she froze in place when she thought about why he was being so much nicer to her lately. Did he think she was the answer to his problems?

CHAPTER SIX

"Be careful," Nick said for the second time as he helped his father into the house. Lenny and Squiggy tried to scoot in before them. He snapped his fingers, and both dogs sat down and waited for their turn.

"I can only be so careful," his father said, and then he coughed several times.

Nick helped him sit in his favorite recliner. His dad was hooked up to an oxygen machine, so Nick set it beside the chair. The dogs settled at his father's feet, as if understanding they were needed there.

"Do you want some water?" he asked, only to be waved away.

"I'm fine, just hand me the remote," his father answered. "Then you can go out and do your chores."

Nick didn't want to leave his dad there alone, but it had been two days and he really needed to check in with his foreman, Daryl Conrad. The man had been working on the Howe ranch since before Nick was born.

Nick and his father trusted Daryl with every detail of running the massive place.

"Call me if—" Nick started, only to have his father wave him away again.

"Don't forget to check in on the Montgomery place," his father called after him as he walked out.

Nick wanted to tell his dad that there was no way he'd forget to go see Kara, but he figured his father already knew that. Was his dad serious about selling the ranch to Wilbert?

How the hell was he supposed to find a wife by Christmas? For the next two hours, he toiled over that question. Every time he thought about it, he came to the same conclusion. Kara.

By the time he rode his horse Bolt towards her ranch, the snow was falling, and he was pretty sure his first step should be to ask her out on a date. Which meant he had to grow a pair of balls on his ride over there.

He was halfway across her field when he noticed her riding towards him from her side field. He pulled Bolt to a halt and waited for her to stop next to him.

"How's your dad?" she asked him, a little breathless. She wore a wool beanie, and her hair was in a thick braid that lay over her shoulder. She had on a heavy coat, gloves, leather chaps over jeans, and riding boots. Her cheeks were pink, showing signs that she'd been riding for some time in the cold.

"At home, resting," he answered. "Out for a ride?"

She nodded. "Care to join us?"

They pulled the horses to fall in step with one another and headed off towards the far field.

"How have things been over here the last few days?" he asked.

"Fine," she answered quickly. "No issues. How are things at your place?"

He shrugged. "Had a busted pipe in the well house. Daryl and the guys fixed it up. Got a few new goats."

She frowned over at him. "Birthed?"

"No, someone dropped them off. Daryl has been letting a few other ranchers know that if they have trouble animals, they can drop them off for rehab."

"You work with goats? Aren't they pretty stupid animals?" She chuckled.

He stilled his horse, and she pulled her horse to a stop too.

"Lady Di would be shocked if she heard you talk about her kind like that," he said, shaking his head.

Kara laughed even more. "You have a goat named Lady Di?"

"She came with the name, and she's as intelligent as... well." He motioned to the horse she was riding. "Whatever her name is."

"James," she supplied, and he smiled and leaned down and took a closer look at the horse.

"Right, sorry ol' chap." He started walking Bolt again. "James and Larry." He shook his head with a chuckle. "Nice names for horses."

"That's Bolt, right?" Kara motioned to his horse.

"Yup." He gave Bolt a pat on the neck.

"James is pretty smart. You're telling me a goat could be as smart as James here?" she asked.

He glanced sideways at her. "We could wager on it?"

She laughed. "Right."

"Chicken?" He egged her on.

She pulled James to a stop again, and he and Bolt had to back step a few steps to be neck and neck with them.

"What kind of wager?" she asked.

"Well, we could run them through simple commands at first."

"No, I mean, what would we bet?" she corrected.

He thought about it. "If I win..."

"If I win, you stop coming around and trying to run the ranch," she interrupted.

He felt like he'd been kicked in the gut. "Trying to get rid of me?" he asked, trying to sound lighthearted.

"No, it's just..." She turned a little pale. "No, it's just..." she said again. "I've waited my entire life to run this place. By myself."

He nodded and took a deep breath. "If I win, you go out on a date with me."

Her eyes went wide.

He held out his gloved hand and waited. She hesitated for a split second, then shook his hand.

"I won't lose. James here is our smartest horse." She lifted her chin slightly.

Nick smiled. "What do you say you ride him over to my place in the morning, and we can see who is smarter. A dumb goat or an old gelding."

She nodded slightly. "First thing in the morning."

He started to turn Bolt back towards his place but stopped when she called after him.

"You... didn't want to come and check up on things at the ranch?" she asked.

He smiled over his shoulder at her. "No, I just came to ask you out on a date." He kicked Bolt into a trot.

He smiled the entire way back home. He took his time making sure Bolt was cooled off. He brushed him, then saw to it that all the animals were safely tucked into the barn for the cold night.

He stopped by Lady Di's pen. She was there waiting for him and the carrot she knew he'd brought her.

"How are you doing tonight, my lady?" he asked, snuggling up to the goat's neck as she munched on the carrot. She let out a happy bleat, then nudged his shoulder. "Okay, okay," he said, pulling out the sugar cube. "Your dessert." He handed it to her, and he could have sworn she smiled at him.

When he walked into the house, his father was sitting at the kitchen table, talking to Stephen McKinney. The man had been his father's lawyer for as long as Nick could remember.

"Evening," he said, running his eyes over his father's face. He was pale, but not as white as before.

"Evening." Stephen stood up and shook Nick's hand. "It looks like we'll get more of the white stuff tonight."

"Yes," Nick answered and motioned to the table. "What's all this?"

"Well," Stephen started.

"I'm updating my will," his father broke in.

"I didn't know you had one," Nick said, walking over and pouring himself a hot cup of coffee. Then he leaned on the counter and waited, knowing his father had something he wanted to say. A point he was making by this show.

"Course I do." His father coughed.

They both waited until his father settled down again.

"Are you sure about these changes?" Stephen asked his dad.

"Sure am." His father glanced over to him. "Go ahead and file it. I think it's what's needed at this point."

Stephen nodded and then stood up again to gather the paperwork. "I'll file it first thing in the morning."

Nick waited until Stephen left before sitting down across from his father.

"You've made your point," he said, looking into his coffee.

"Have I?" his father asked, coughing. "Tell me you've at least asked the girl out."

Nick thought about the bet and realized that if Lady Di lost tomorrow, he'd not only lose his chance to go out with her, but he'd also have to stop going over to the ranch as an excuse each day.

"See." His father thumped the table. "That is exactly why I'm forced to make the next move for you." He pointed towards the door where Stephen had just left.

"How did you know Mom was the one?" he asked, deciding to change tactics.

His father softened, then let out a loud breath. "The moment I first saw your ma, I knew," he answered. "My heart jumped in my chest, my palms got so sweaty I swore I was going to drop my tools." He smiled. "Then she looked up at me and our eyes met." His father closed his eyes and Nick watched a tear slide down his cheek. "I waited too damn long to ask her out. Too damn long before I asked her to marry me. And too damn long to have you." He opened his eyes and pointed at him. "Don't make the same mistakes I made." His father started to stand up and Nick moved to help, but his father held up his hand. "Stay. I'm going to lie down for a bit before supper. Think about what I've said. I'd sure hate for Wilbert and his boy to get their grubby hands on this place."

"Then don't change your will."

A strange look crossed his father's eyes just before he turned around and walked out of the room without saying anything further.

Nick sat at the table and nursed the coffee before getting up to make them dinner.

He went to bed that night thinking over what he would do if Lady Di lost. By morning, he'd come up with a backup plan. If his goat lost, he'd have to beg Kara to go out on a date with him.

CHAPTER SEVEN

Kara leaned on the edge of the paddock and watched in amazement as the pure white goat navigated the snow-covered grassy area and obeyed each and every one of Nick's commands.

First, Lady Di bowed to Nick, then moved around him to the left in a full circle before turning and going around him to the right. She jumped up on her hind legs and danced around before bowing again. Then Nick had the goat standing on her hind legs and doing twirls. Kara watched as Lady Di jumped over his legs and even through a hoop he had.

There were even obstacles set up in the paddock that the goat easily maneuvered around when prompted, jumping between overturned barrels to an old tire. Someone, probably Nick, had built a wooden bridge between a stack of pallets and an old picnic table. The goat happily walked across it when motioned to do so.

They ended the show-off session when Nick bent over and Lady Di jumped onto his back and shoulders. Then she actually kissed him on the chin, making them both laugh.

"Well?" he asked when the goat was back down on the ground. "What'd you think?"

She smiled as Lady Di walked over to her to get attention.

"I think," she looked up at Nick, "that I just lost a bet."

He laughed as he leaned on the fence. "James doesn't know how to jump through hoops?"

She shook her head. "James can bow and dance. That's about it."

"That's a pretty neat trick. For a dumb horse," he joked, and she smiled again.

She stood up when Lady Di walked over to get some water. Nick was standing so close to her, she lost her breath for a few seconds. Even though the fence separated them, she could smell his aftershave, a rich musky scent that had her knees going weak.

She leaned heavier on the rail of the fence.

"So..." He smiled. "How about tomorrow night?"

She blinked a few times, trying to clear her foggy mind. "Tomorrow?"

"You lost the bet. You aren't going to chicken out, are you?" he teased.

"Chicken..." She thought. The date. She'd lost the bet. He'd wagered a date with her. He'd won. "Oh," she said and swallowed hard. What would it be like, being seen in town with Nick? Would everyone assume they were an item or just two friends casually eating dinner together? She knew how little towns were. She'd gone to lunch with a high school friend once and word had spread so fast that they were an item, the guy had purposely made fun of her in front of his friends so that he wouldn't be associated with her in a romantic sense.

"I was thinking, since I need to stick close to the ranch

because of my dad's health, that you could come over here tomorrow night for dinner," Nick said.

"Oh," she said again. "Sure." She bit her bottom lip.

Did that mean he didn't want to be seen in public with her? Maybe he too was questioning being seen with her?

That couldn't be it. They'd just had breakfast at the diner yesterday morning. Then again, everyone in town knew that his father was in the hospital. They would assume that she was just being a good—

"You're overthinking it," Nick said, breaking into her thoughts. "I can see your brain working overtime." He laid his hand over hers. "Kara, I want to go out with you," he said softly. "But I need to stick close to my dad." He shook his head and took a deep breath. "When we can, I'd like to take you out somewhere nice."

She felt her heart kick in her chest and smiled back at him. "I'd like that." And the truth was, she meant it.

"Good," he said, and then he surprised her by leaning over the fence a little more. "Then you won't mind if I..." He dropped off as he brushed his lips across hers.

The kiss was so soft, so smooth, so... damn sexy that she wanted more. She needed more.

He leaned back just a couple inches, and his eyes searched hers. Had his eyes always been the color of coffee just the way she liked it? Dark and rich, but with a swirl of caramel.

As if in slow motion, his hand came up and cupped her face, drawing her closer until her eyes slid closed as he pressed his lips against hers again, this time a little more firmly.

He even tasted like coffee. Rich and full of dreamy flavors she could spend hours exploring. His fingers tangled in her hair, pressing to the back of her neck ever so lightly. If she wanted to, she could jerk away, but instead, she pressed herself to him and, feeling a loose nail dig into her side, realized that the fence was still between them.

She jerked back slightly when she felt the sting of the nail.

"Oh," Nick said, looking down. "Damn, I meant to nail that in." He took the hem of her shirt in his hands. "It's torn."

She looked down at it, not caring. Then he lifted the hem up to check her skin, and she felt her entire body heat at the thought of him removing all of her clothes.

What was wrong with her? This was Nick. This was... the boy of her dreams who had turned into the man of her dreams right before her eyes. Somehow, she hadn't even realized how much she'd wanted him. How much she'd grown to like him. What he meant to her.

"It doesn't look like the nail broke the skin," Nick said, looking back up into her eyes. "Are you okay?"

She nodded, not really wanting to open her mouth for fear of what might come falling out.

"Good," he said. He easily jumped the fence and landed by her side. He took her hand, and they started walking towards James. "Since you're here and James is here..." He stopped and turned towards her. "How about I saddle up Crash, and we head out for a ride?"

She nodded again.

"Good." He smiled and took her hand again, only this time, they headed towards the barn.

When they stepped inside, she stopped and gaped at the space.

"Wow." She blinked to let her eyes adjust so she could get a better look.

The Howe's ranch house was a beautiful sight. The home was easily twice the size of her family home. It was made of wood and glass and sat on top of a small hillside. The back of the home had large windows that overlooked the Howe property. The long drive split in two near the road, and a dirt lane headed off in the direction of a few trailers and a smaller ranch house. She knew that a few full-time staff lived out there, most of them in the trailers or in campers of their own. She'd always been told to steer clear of them, since most of them were drifters.

She'd only been inside the Howe home twice over the years. Once, when Nick's mother died and the other when his father had been really sick, and her stepmother had delivered a casserole.

Kara didn't know why she hadn't been in there more often, but then again, Nick had probably only been inside her home a handful of times too.

The barn impressed her and made her immediately jealous. From the outside, the building looked like any other barn. It was tan, with a dark metal roof. There were thick wood beams holding up a long section of roofing that sat directly over the outside paddock areas.

Inside the barn, there were at least a dozen stalls on one side of the building, all made of the same wide wood beams and black iron railings. On the other side was a wall of doors. Some were large garage-style doors and others were smaller and led into storerooms.

Compared to her small barn, which housed three horses and had barely any storage area, this was a mansion for animals.

"This is impressive," she said, following him to a stall.

Each of the horses had their names carved into wood plaques that hung above the stall doors.

"Crash, Bolt, Lightning, Thunder, and..." She moved down to see the last horse. "Mariann?"

Nick chuckled. "She's not really part of the family. I'm breaking her in for the Bertons."

"Right." She smiled and nodded to his horses. "I see a theme. Do you name all your animals after a stormy night?"

He chuckled. "Just the horses. The cattle are named after Pokémon."

"Gotta catch 'em all." She smiled and he nodded.

"The chickens are named after Star Wars characters." He walked over and opened a door. Inside was a room filled with saddles and other riding gear. He took a saddle and set it down on a bench, then walked over and got Crash out. She leaned against the door to his stall and watched as he saddled him.

"What about the goats?" she asked.

"Most of them came with names. Next generation is going to be Star Trek characters." He smiled. "First and second generation."

She laughed. "Nerd."

"You know it." He smiled.

"What about football or basketball players?" she asked.

He shrugged. "I only played in those sports to piss off Willy by being better than him," he admitted, and she laughed.

"I knew it." She pointed towards him. "Everyone did, actually."

"I think at one point it was common knowledge." He tightened the saddle.

"Is that why you dated Carla in tenth grade?" she asked, remembering the hot redhead that Willy had bragged he was going to bang before prom.

"No, I dated her to protect her from Willy."

"He hates being called that," she said with a smile. "Which is why I call him that all the time."

Nick chuckled. "Me too."

Nick finished getting Crash ready for the ride and then helped her get back on James before they set out across the field.

She figured he would want to stick close to the house, and sure enough they made a large circle around the property. While they rode, they talked about Willy and everything he'd done over the years to get back at Nick.

"It's like he has a playbook and is going through different moves to see what works," Nick said with a chuckle.

"I wish he'd give up trying with me," she admitted with a sigh.

"Is he still bothering you?" Nick asked with a frown.

"No, not for a while, but that won't stop him from trying again. He usually forgets about me for chunks at a time. Then something will set him off and, boom, he's knocking on my door again." She rolled her eyes.

Nick was frowning so much now that she decided to change the subject to the animals that he was training. By the time they returned to the barn, they were both laughing again as the snow started falling. The sky had turned gray and there was a bite to the wind now.

She started to tie James up outside so she could help Nick put Crash away, but he stopped her by taking her hand in his.

"No, I've got this. You should go home before it gets too bad out here." Nick rubbed her ungloved hands in his. "I already kept you out in the cold too long."

"You didn't keep me," she pointed out.

"Here." He stepped inside the barn and came back with

a pair of warm riding gloves. "You shouldn't go out riding without a pair."

"Thanks." She held onto them, wishing he'd hold her hands again instead.

"Tomorrow night. I'll pick you up around six," he said, leaning back against the barn door.

"I could—" she started, but he shook his head.

"I'll pick you up," he said with a smile. Then he walked over to her and pulled her close again. "So it will be an official date," he said quietly. Her entire body warmed next to his. "Go home, Kara." He brushed his lips across hers, then helped her back into the saddle. She wanted to argue with him, but she slid on the gloves and turned James towards home.

CHAPTER EIGHT

Nick watched Kara and James disappear through the falling snow. He waited until they were just dots going into the barn across the field before he took Crash's saddle off and brushed the horse down.

When he stepped into the house, his father was lying on the sofa, fast asleep. His snoring could wake the dead, but Nick sat on the recliner next to him and enjoyed every moment of it.

The following morning, his father's health took a turn. Nick wanted to call the doctor, but his father refused.

Nick finally convinced the old man to stay in bed and served him both breakfast and lunch there. His father hardly ate a bite.

For dinner, Nick had planned on serving Kara some grilled steaks. There was a large freezer in the work room off the back of the house that held all of their meat. Each and every bit was from their own cattle, pigs, and chickens.

The storeroom held some of the vegetable crops from their land and some of the canned apples and pears from the small orchard. One of the first things his mother had taught him was how to can fruits and vegetables. The room also held many jars of homemade jelly.

"You'll need this skill someday when you take over the ranch," she had told him so many times. Each year since her death, he'd canned as much as he could. One year, he'd gotten it in his brain to try making homemade ketchup. Since then, he'd never bought it and even planted more tomatoes the following year to keep up with the demand from him and his father through the winter months.

What would he do next season when his father wasn't around? In the past few years, ever since his dad's first battle with cancer, he hadn't helped out all that much. Still, his old man took care of most of the finances—making sure the taxes were paid on time, paying the employees.

Even after Nick had transferred the accounting to an online application, his father still sat at the computer once a month and ran over the figures. Nick was the one signing the checks now, since his father's handwriting was too shaky to read.

What was he going to do without the old man around? He glanced around the kitchen. The place was going to seem so lonely.

When his phone alarm went off, he rushed up the stairs to shower and get dressed for his date. After poking his head into his father's room, he headed out to pick up Kara.

The drive down his driveway and back up hers took less than five minutes. Still, his nerves doubled in that short time.

The snow hadn't let up all day, which meant that the driveways were a mess, which is why he'd driven his truck instead of the sedan. He knocked on the door and thought he heard a bang and a curse, which had him smiling.

"Coming," Kara called out, and he heard a door slam and footsteps before the door opened.

She was wearing a pair of black jeans, boots, and a big white sweater. Her long hair was curled and lying over her shoulders.

She looked so perfect, his insides ached.

"Hi," he said as he smiled.

"Hi." She smiled back at him. "We are sure getting a lot of snow lately." She grabbed her coat.

"It's supposed to clear up this weekend," he said, helping her put on her coat. "Ready?"

She glanced around the house and then turned back to him and nodded.

He opened the truck door for her and then got behind the wheel.

"How is your dad doing?" she asked as they made their way back to his place.

"He's... bedridden now. As of this morning. I'm not sure he'll make it to Christmas."

"Is there anything I can do?"

He shook his head. "No, he's made it very clear he wants to go be with my mom. He's arranged for everything." He hesitated for a split second and then added, "He's even changed his will."

She was quiet for a heartbeat and then said, "There's a rumor going around town."

He groaned. "Yeah, I've heard it."

"Is it true?"

He glanced at her and shrugged. "I don't know. I haven't asked my dad. Nor am I going to. What he's decided to do is his business."

"Even if it leaves you homeless?" she asked.

He thought about it and nodded. "If my father has

decided to leave the ranch to my uncle or his son, then it's his business. I've worked hard all my life for this place," he said as he turned into the long driveway. "I believe my father knows this. He's a good man. He knows what's best for it and me." He parked and shut off the truck. "But don't get me wrong. If it's within my power, I'll fight for this place, just as I'm sure you'll fight for yours."

She smiled and nodded.

He jumped out and rushed around to help her out of the truck. As they stepped inside, the dogs happily greeted them.

"Something smells good," she said as he helped her off with her coat.

"I figured I'd go with a classic. Steak and potatoes followed up with homemade apple pie." He smiled as he hung their coats on the hook by the front door.

Then he noticed her eyes scanning the room.

"Is this your first time in here?" he asked.

"No, but it's the first I've had time to look around."

He motioned to the space. "I'll go check on the food." He disappeared through the large two-story living room.

The kitchen was easily twice the size as the one in her house. His mother had put in state-of-the-art appliances, but that had been over ten years ago. Still, they worked and were nice enough. Over the years, he and his dad had repainted most of the inside. There were a lot of natural wood beams, which kept the painting requirements down.

The old hardwood flooring had been sanded and restained many times and still looked new.

"Wow."

He turned to see Kara standing just inside the kitchen hallway.

"You like?" he asked, motioning her into the room.

"This is... no wonder you can cook." She shook her head and chuckled. "With a kitchen like this, I'd learn to cook too."

"This room is all my mother's doing. She spent more hours in here than any other room. She's the one who taught me how to cook, bake, and can."

She turned to him, a surprised look on his face. "You know how to can foods?"

He smiled and, as an answer, walked over to the huge walk-in pantry and opened the door. "See for yourself. I made everything in there." He motioned around after turning on the light.

She stepped past him slowly and into the pantry. Each of the four walls were lined with shelves that were stocked with everything from homemade applesauce to canned zucchini.

"You have everything alphabetized?" She turned to look at him.

He shrugged. "My mother set up the system. I just kept it. It works."

Her fingers traced over the rows and rows of jelly he'd made. "You make Florence's Jams?" She held up a jar and showed him. "I bought some at the farmer's market."

He nodded and felt a pinch in his heart that always happened when he saw his mother's name on the label.

"Yes. My mother's name was Florence."

She gasped slightly and then held the jar to her heart as if protecting it. "I... I'm sorry."

He shrugged and walked over to place his hand on her shoulder lightly. "Keep the jar. Take more if you want."

He thought about losing it all, losing everything in this room to his uncle and cousin, and felt his stomach turn. "Come on, dinner will be ready."

"Nick." Kara stopped him by putting a hand on his arm. "Your mother would be very proud of you. I remember how much she loved you. You were lucky to have as much time with her as you did."

He remembered that her mother had died before she and her father had moved there. She'd spent years without a mother before her father had finally remarried. He couldn't imagine growing up and not having his mother there, even for the short amount of time he'd had her.

Nodding, he took her free hand and walked back out into the kitchen.

"I set the dining room table." He walked her through the kitchen. "There's some wine chilling, but if you want—"

"Wine is good," she said as they stepped into the dining room.

"Sit," he said, pulling out the chair. "I'll pour some wine, and you can sip it while I grab the food."

She sat down, setting the jar next to her plate. He'd done everything except light the candles, which he did now.

"This is very nice," she said, after taking a sip of the wine. Her eyes narrowed slightly. "You didn't make it, did you?"

He laughed. "No, I draw the line at fermenting anything." She smiled. "I did try making some currant wine once." He visibly shivered. "It didn't go well."

He left her laughing as he went into the kitchen to plate the meal, which he'd left warming in the oven.

After poking his head into his father's room to make sure he was okay, he took the plates into the dining room and sat down.

"Wow, okay, some serious chef skills," Kara said after the first bite. "Why hasn't anyone tied you down?"

He smiled. "I just haven't found the one that I want to tie me down. How about you?"

"I'm married to the ranch," she said between bites. "Besides, you know what's available in this town." She rolled her eyes. "Other than Willy and his gang, there's..." She tilted her head as if she was thinking. Then she shrugged. "There's about five other men, most of whom are either married or..." She shook her head. "Nope, they are either part of Willy's gang or married."

"Not all guys in town fall into those two categories," he said.

Her eyebrows shot up. "Name one. Besides you," she added quickly.

He thought about it. Thought back to all the guys in his class. Few of them, except for the handful that hung out with Willy, had stuck around. The ones that had stayed had married their high school girlfriends shortly after graduation. Then he thought to the classes before and after his.

"Todd," he said quickly. "He works down at the hardware store."

"Todd?" She laughed. "Todd Brewer?"

"Yes." He lifted his chin. "He's not married and doesn't hang out with Willy."

"But he is gay," she said with a little head nod. "You knew that, right?"

He frowned. "Todd is not..." He dropped off and suddenly everything made sense. The man always went out of his way to help Nick whenever he was in the store.

Kara smiled. "Don't worry. He hasn't officially come out yet." She leaned her elbow on the table and lifted her eyebrows. "Anyone else you can think of?"

He frowned as he ran through names and faces.

"Okay, you've got me," he finally admitted. "I can't think of a single one."

"That's because there aren't any." She leaned back and took another sip of her wine. "Liz and I have gone through all our yearbooks. No one stuck around Cedar. If they did, they got married within the first year out of school."

"You're telling me you haven't dated since school?"

She shook her head. "I went out once or twice, but it was with guys from Casper."

"What about Liz?" he asked. "She's dated a few guys from town."

"Nope. She may brag about it, but most of them she met on a dating app and they are from Casper as well," Kara answered. "Trust me, men are scarce in this town. Unlike women. I bet you have at least two dozen women our age to pick from. Most of them stuck around town after graduation."

He thought about it and could easily name at least a dozen women he could take out. He'd gone out on dates with at least three in the past year alone.

"Okay, Cedar is really not equal in that area," he admitted. "At least you have me." He held up his wine glass towards her.

"Until you find someone to fall in love with," she said, tapping her glass against his.

He frowned. "Who says I won't fall in love with you?"

Her eyes narrowed, and she leaned forward slightly. "How much wine have you had?"

He set his glass down. Did she really not feel that way towards him? Not even the slightest? Maybe she was only here tonight on the makeshift date because she'd lost the bet.

"What would be so bad about..." He waved between them.

She opened her mouth to answer, but just then there was a loud crash from his father's room. He jumped up and rushed down the hallway, spilling the glass of wine he'd just set down.

The red liquid seeped into his mother's rug and stained the material. A mark he would always look at and remember just how his first date with Kara had ended.

CHAPTER NINE

Kara stood in the Howe's living room three days later. Only this time, the place was filled with townspeople she knew. The smell of food carried in from the kitchen. The hodgepodge of aromas made her stomach turn slightly.

What she needed was air. Glancing around to make sure no one was paying attention to her, she slipped through the crowd and stepped out onto the back deck unnoticed.

The snow had stopped, and the sun was warming the fields. Only a few patches of snow remained on the silhouetted hills, where the sun hadn't hit.

In the darkness of the shadows, the air was crisp, unforgivingly cold. But the sun shone on the back of the house, and she leaned against the railing, taking a deep breath of the cool air while the rays warmed her.

"How are you holding up?"

Kara jumped slightly and turned to see Nick leaning against the back wall of the house, in the shadows. His arms were crossed over his chest. He looked like he'd been there a while.

"Me?" She stood straight and ran her eyes over him. He was wearing a suit but had removed the tie he'd been wearing earlier that day at his father's funeral. "How about you?"

"You look tired," he said, not paying any attention to her words.

"I'm fine," she said, worried about him. He looked... lost. "Have you eaten anything?"

His eyes closed for a moment. "I just got done meeting with my father's lawyer."

She wanted to go to him, but she just wrapped her arms around herself to ward off the chill that suddenly hit her. Even though she was wearing a black sweater dress, the sun's rays suddenly weren't enough to keep her warm.

"And?" she asked.

He stood up straight and moved to stand next to her. His eyes scanned the horizon.

"The will is to be read on Christmas Day." He sighed before looking over at her.

She frowned. "Christmas?"

He took another deep breath. "You're cold. Let's go in."

She stopped him from walking away by laying her hand on his arm. "Nick. Talk to me." Her eyes scanned his but only found sadness there.

Suddenly the back door burst open, and Wilbert strolled through it, followed closely by Willy.

"There you are, my boy." Wilbert smiled brightly and walked over to slap Nick on the shoulder.

The man's attitude the entire day was that of pure joy, even though his brother had just died.

"Uncle," Nick said with a strained tone.

"I think it's time we did ourselves some business." Wilbert glanced towards Kara. "Willy, why don't you keep

Miss Montgomery company while my nephew and I have ourselves a little chat."

Willy smiled and moved over to throw an arm over Kara's shoulders and pulled her in tight to his chest. Kara would have kneed the guy, but the entire town was standing on the other side of the windows, watching the show.

Nick dislodged his uncle's hand from his shoulder and walked over to them. Willy removed his arm, and Kara stepped closer towards Nick.

"Any discussion we may need to have can wait until tomorrow," Nick said firmly. He took Kara's hand in his, and she followed him as he started to walk inside.

"Tomorrow then, boy. I'll be knocking on the door bright and early," Wilbert said loudly behind them.

"What was that all about?" Kara asked Nick when they stepped inside.

"Nothing," he mumbled. "Let's get you some food."

Nick was surrounded by well-wishers while she shuffled off to get a plate of food with Liz.

"This is crazy," Liz said when they'd found a place to sit down, each of them balancing a paper plate of food on their knees.

"What is?" Kara asked after taking a bite of a roll. Her stomach was still upset, and she didn't want to push her luck eating something that might cause her to rush home and be sick.

"The fact that the entire town can fit in this house," Liz answered as she motioned to the room with her drumstick before taking a bite out of it.

"I don't think the entire town is here," Kara said.

"Oh, I'm pretty sure they are. Everyone knew and loved Nicholas Howe. Did you know he donated money to pretty much every charity in town? Not to mention he helped build the new library."

Kara nodded. "Yeah." She did know. The man was as generous as he was kind.

Liz leaned closer and lowered her voice. "It's going to be crazy if Wilbert and Willy get their hands on this place."

"I don't think they will," Kara said, setting down her half-eaten roll.

"Rumors—" Liz started.

"Are just that. Rumors," Kara pointed out. "Let's let things settle before starting any more."

Liz pouted for a moment then cheered up. "So, is it true then?"

"Is what true?" Kara asked.

"That you were with Nick when his father passed?" Liz asked.

Kara held in a groan. "Yes, I was here."

Her friend's blonde eyebrows shot up. "Doing?"

"Having dinner," Kara said, glancing around the room for any signs of Nick.

Liz nudged her knee with her own, almost dislodging Kara's paper plate.

"Hey," Kara said, nudging her friend's knee back.

"Doing what?" Liz hissed.

"I lost a bet," she admitted, not sure she wanted it all over town that her first date with Nick had ended in a death. She was looking at her friend when Liz's eyes turned to a person standing in front of them.

Kara turned her head slightly to see Nick standing directly in front of her.

When her eyes met his, she could see hurt join the sorrow.

"I..." Nick started but turned to leave.

Kara dumped her plate on her friends lap and followed Nick through the house, finally catching up with him at the base of the stairs.

"Hey," she said, taking his hand. "Are you okay?"

He refused to look at her, and she had to tug on his arm to get him to turn around.

"I'm not sure how to get everyone to leave," he said, not giving her a chance to speak.

She swallowed the apology she'd wanted to give him. Was he hurt that she hadn't told her friend they had been on a date? It hadn't really been a real date. Had it?

"I can help," she said, wanting to smooth things over with him.

He glanced back towards the living room and nodded, still avoiding her eyes.

"Nick?" she said, looking down at their joined hands. "I—"

Just then there was a loud bang followed by a couple shouts.

They rushed down the hallway to the kitchen, where Willy stood over Daryl, who was laid out on the kitchen floor with a bloodied lip.

"You're the help," Willy shouted. "You don't talk to the boss like that."

Nick rushed to Daryl's side and bent to help the man up.

Out of all the hired hands, Daryl Conrad was the only one that Kara knew and liked. The man had always been at Howe Ranch. He was older than Nicholas had been but in far better physical health.

"Out." Nick made a sound close to a growl. She'd never heard anything like it from him before.

"Yeah, you heard that, nigger, you'd better—" Willy

started, but Nick stood up quickly and went nose to nose with his cousin.

"I said, get out," Nick said in a low tone. "If you ever talk to anyone on this property like that again..."

Nick's fists clenched, and she swore she saw Willy wince.

"You'll what?" Wilbert walked into the room.

Nick didn't even spare the older man a glance. "Daryl, would you like to press charges?" Nick asked.

"No." Daryl stood up and took Nick's shoulders. "We all know it wouldn't do any good."

Nick turned to Wilbert finally. "Get your son out of here. When you come back to talk business, leave him at home. Where he belongs." Nick turned back to Daryl and ran his eyes over the man's face. "Maybe Kara can help you clean up?" he asked, and she rushed forward to take Daryl's arm.

"Come on," she said, pulling the older man along with her.

"Out," Nick said firmly again, this time to the crowd watching the show. "Everyone. The party's over." He motioned towards the front of the house while she and Daryl walked into a bathroom.

For the next few minutes, she helped the older man clean up his bloody lip. They could hear the sounds of the entire town leaving Nick's house.

"I didn't do nothing to provoke that kid," Daryl said with a sigh. "That one's just... off."

"Yeah, he is," Kara agreed as she wiped the man's bloody lip.

"I can do this, myself. It's not the first time I've been bloodied. Nor, I fear, the last." Daryl smiled.

"Nick asked me to help." She smiled up at him.

"Besides, I think he wants to make sure you didn't bump your head."

"I didn't." Daryl sighed. "The kid punches like the child he is."

Kara laughed as the house grew quiet.

"How are you holding up, old timer?" Nick asked from the doorway.

"Shadow did me worse just last week," Daryl joked. "That horse is going to be the death of me. Mark my words."

"You say that about every horse you break." Nick's smile was fast and over before she could fully enjoy the view of it. "I think there are a lot of leftovers in the kitchen. You should take some out to the boys. I'm sure they'd appreciate the pies," Nick suggested.

Daryl stood up and rubbed his hands together. "I was just heading into the kitchen to get me a slice of that rhubarb pie anyway."

Daryl quickly disappeared, leaving them alone in the bathroom. Kara turned and started cleaning the mess she'd made.

"You can leave that," Nick said behind her.

She dumped the tissue into the trash and turned to him.

"I didn't mean what I said earlier," she blurted out. Nick's dark eyebrows rose in question. "About the other night just being a bet."

Nick seemed to relax slightly. "Okay."

"I mean..." She leaned against the sink and crossed her arms over her chest. "I didn't come over just because of the bet."

Nick's eyes moved to her mouth as she licked her lips in frustration.

"What did it mean?" he asked, moving closer to her.

Her breath hitched as her eyes lowered to his lips,

remembering what it had done to her when he kissed her. She wanted to feel that way again.

"What did it mean to you?" she asked, her voice breathless, like she'd just run through the fields.

"Kara." Nick's hands took her shoulders. "This... means something." He pulled her into his arms. "I can't think straight. Not yet. But... I just want you to know that."

She held onto him and closed her eyes tightly as she listened to his heartbeat next to her ear.

Then, just as quickly as he'd held onto her, he pulled back. She instantly missed the feeling of him. The sound of his heartbeat.

"Thanks for helping out." He turned to leave the room. "Feel free to take some leftovers."

"Nick?" she said, and he paused at the door.

"I'll be over after my meeting with my uncle," he said when she didn't say anything more. Then he walked out of the bathroom, leaving her shaking and wanting.

The next morning, she woke and ate half-burned waffles and coffee before checking on all the animals.

When she walked outside, she noticed a truck parked outside of Nick's place and wondered what they were talking about while she completed her chores.

"Oh, to be a fly on the wall," she told Wilbur, who had turned into a rather agreeable pig since Nick had worked with him. Wilbur looked up at her from his slop and oinked loudly at her in agreement. She was thankful that Liz's dad had informed her he'd already bought a wild turkey from his neighbor, who had killed two on a hunting trip. "You know, maybe I'll just bring turkey for Christmas this year," she said, sitting on the edge of the fence as she watched the pig.

"I bet he likes to hear that," Nick said from a few feet away, causing her to squeal and almost fall off the fence.

"Jesus, Mary, and Joseph! Don't sneak up on someone like that." Kara held her hand over her heart until it settled down in her chest.

Nick chuckled and moved over to stand next to her, leaning on the fence and looking down at Wilbur.

"If you'd been paying attention, you would have seen me riding across the field towards you." He motioned to Crash, who was tied up just outside the barn.

"Right," she said and took a deep breath. "How'd things go with your uncle?"

"Until the official reading of my father's will... things are strained," Nick answered.

She frowned. "What did the lawyer tell you yesterday?"

"He was there to tell me that my father requested his will not be read until Christmas Day," he answered. "That was all."

"He can do that?"

"Lawyers will do anything their client's request. If they're paid enough. Naturally, my uncle thinks this is a good sign. He wants to make a deal with me before the will is read."

"A deal?"

"He wants the ranch. He's pretty sure my father left it to him if I wasn't married before my father's death."

"Which you aren't." She sighed, then turned to him. "You aren't, are you?" She smiled.

He smiled back at her. "Nope."

"Are you sure you didn't sneak off to Vegas and marry a stripper?" she teased.

He shook his head. "I've never been to Vegas."

Her eyebrows arched. "You haven't? You should go sometime."

"And marry a stripper?" he teased back.

"Hey, they're just working girls," she pointed out.

"True, but I don't think any stripper would be comfortable living out here in the middle of nowhere in a small town, on a ranch." He motioned to the pig. "Taking care of farm animals."

She laughed. "You never know. I'd wager there are a few that would love to live on a ranch, have a handsome husband who can cook and can foods, not to mention make homemade jelly." She wiggled her eyebrows at him.

His smile slipped slightly, and his eyes dipped to her lips again.

"Kara."

Just hearing her name come from his lips had her heart racing again. She jumped for a second time when her cell phone rang loudly in her pocket.

Seeing her father's number on the screen, she sighed before answering the call.

"Hey, Daddy, how's the trip going?" She jumped down from the fence and walked away from the noise of the barn animals.

"Good, sweetie. We just heard about Nicholas," her father said.

Kara glanced to where Nick was talking softly to Wilbur.

"Yeah, the services were yesterday."

"I hope you had flowers delivered for us," her father said.

"Yes, I did."

"How's Nick holding up?"

She glanced at Nick again. "He's holding up. He's here right now."

"He is?" Her father said something to Luanna as he held his hand over the phone, but she still heard it perfectly.

"Nick's there with her right now." Luanna answered, "Well, get off the phone and leave them alone. This is just what we planned."

When her father came back, she asked, "What did you have planned? What does that mean?"

Her father was quiet for a moment, then he said, "Um, honey, I can't... hear you..." and hung up.

She frowned down at her phone and was about to call them back when she realized Nick was watching her.

"How about a ride?" she asked him. "The sun is finally out, and I want to exercise Bella."

CHAPTER TEN

Everything was up in the air. His entire life was hanging by a thread. He should be more worried than he was, but in truth, in the back of his mind and in his heart, he knew that his father had ensured the safety of his future.

There was no doubt of his father's love. There never had been. He'd been lucky enough to be raised by two people who loved one another and him. Unconditionally.

That love had been the foundation of his life, which had allowed him to grow into the man he was today.

Unlike his cousin, Nick had been raised to work for what he had. For as long as he could remember, he'd worked the ranch. Long hard days side by side with both of his parents.

When his mother had been alive, he'd split his time working with his dad or working with his mother. After his mother's death, he'd taken over all the duties she'd done around the property. His father's health had forced him to slide into both roles over the past few years.

Could his uncle Wilbert, his aunt Marge, and Willy

ever fill those roles? Did they know just how much work went into running the hundred-acre place?

"You're very quiet over there." Kara's voice broke into his thoughts.

He glanced over at her. They were walking the horses along a well-traveled path around her property line. The sun was shining on her face, turning her cheeks a shade of pink that flattered her very much. Her hair was tied in a long braid that lay over her shoulder.

She looked like a rancher. Strong. Healthy. Beautiful.

"Just thinking about the future," he answered. "Have you ever wondered where you'll be twenty years from now?"

She smiled. "Sure, I'll be right here." She motioned with her chin. "Why would I want to leave paradise?"

He smiled at her answer. "No big city dreams? You once mentioned wanting to move away. College in Denver, I believe it was."

She laughed. "I was a child." She rolled her eyes.

"Was?" he joked and had her laughing.

"What about you? Did you ever want to leave?" she asked.

He thought about it. "Travel, yes, but leave?" He shook his head. "I supposed after my injuries, I couldn't imagine being anywhere but here." He motioned with his head towards his land.

She was quiet for a moment. "What will you do if..."

"I don't know," he said when she didn't finish the question. "I guess I haven't thought that far ahead. I still believe in my heart that my father wouldn't leave me high and dry."

"I'm sure you're right," she agreed. "He loved you very much." She reached across the space and touched his arm.

He felt so much lighter at her words. It was as if having her confirm his thoughts solidified them.

"What do you say we let these two get some real exercise?" He motioned towards the horses.

"A race?" Kara's eyebrows rose.

"Sure," he agreed.

"Are you going to bet me another date?" she teased.

He smiled. "This time, whoever wins gets to pick the place we go."

She nodded, then glanced around and nodded. "To the old oak?"

"You're on," he agreed and then laughed when she kicked Bella's sides and had the horse sprinting away, leaving him and Crash behind.

In the end, they were neck to neck when they stopped under the large oak tree. They walked for a while to let them rest as they talked about the town and what had happened the day before between Daryl and Willy.

He knew that Willy and Wilbert had always had a problem with Daryl. According to them, the man lived on the ranch rent-free and was nothing more than a squatter.

They, of course, didn't see all the man did for the property. Daryl worked three hundred and sixty-five days a year. Sometimes ten to twelve hour shifts. All because he wanted to, not because he had to.

His father had tried to give Daryl vacations every year, but the man always spent his time off doing what he loved the best—working the land and helping the animals.

Nick didn't know if Daryl had any family. He had at one point had an old dog named Scratch. When the dog had died, Daryl claimed it was too hard on him to get another to replace his best friend. Instead, he'd thrown himself into his work and had spent more time training horses with Nick.

His father had never charged Daryl a dime for rent, yet the man continued to drop a check off each month for the old ranch house he lived in. At this point, his father should have just given him the place and the land it sat on. The man had earned it.

"I never figured your uncle and cousin as racists," Kara said as they reached the barn.

"They're a lot of things," he admitted as they turned the corner. Glancing towards his place, he noticed a truck in front of his house. "I'd better go see who that is." He motioned to his home.

She frowned and followed his gaze. "Need help?"

"No. I'm sorry I won't be able to help you out today around here."

She waved him off. "Go. We'll have time to talk later on our date," she said with a smile. "I'll pick where you're taking me."

He laughed, feeling better than he had in days. He kicked Crash into a trot heading home.

When he reached the gate that separated his property from Kara's, he could see that the truck was a newer model. It still had temporary tags on it, and there was a horse trailer attached to the back.

Whoever it was had opened the barn door and was inside.

When he dismounted from Crash, Willy stepped out of the barn, holding the reins of Bolt, leading the horse out towards the trailer.

"What the hell do you think you're doing with my horse?" he asked, tying Crash's reins off before storming over to Willy.

"Just cleaning the place out," Willy said, jerking the

reins away from him. "Pa told me to have the place empty by the time he gets here."

"I don't give a fuck what your father said. This is my property. My horse." Nick reached up and took Bolt's reins back. The horse, now completely spooked, jerked his head several times.

He marched over and tied Bolt next to Crash, letting both horses settled down.

The meeting with his uncle had been pretty much what he'd thought it would be. His uncle demanding Nick move out of his property, even though the will hadn't been read yet. In the end, he'd thought he'd convinced his uncle to leave everything alone until after the will had been read. His uncle had stormed out, and Nick had thought that was the end of it.

"You're just putting off the inevitable," Willy said, heading back into the barn.

Nick was on his heels and stopped him from opening Thunder's stall door.

Willy spun on his heels and caught Nick off guard. The first punch to the jaw hadn't hurt. The second one to the eye did. By the time Willy swung at him a third time, Nick was ready and easily ducked and swung back.

His first hit Willy in the jaw, hard enough that his cousin flew back against the stall door before sinking to the cement floor.

"You did it. My pa is going to have everything now," Willy spewed. He spit blood as he started to get up.

"Stay put," he warned and pulled out his phone. He dialed 911 and as he started to relay what had happened, Willy pulled out his phone and called his father.

By the time the police showed up, Nick's left eye was swollen shut and he had finally got his lip to stop bleeding.

Willy had a red jaw and was arguing with his father when the police arrived.

Gary Laird and Kyle Morgan were two of his father's old buddies. But both men knew Wilbert as well.

When they started walking towards Nick, Wilbert stepped in front of him and held up his hands as if to stop him.

"Thanks for coming out, Gary, Kyle." Wilbert nodded to each man. "I'm here now and can..."

Nick sidestepped his uncle and broke in.

"Willy was trying to steal my horses." He motioned to Bolt and then the trailer. "He told me his father wanted the place cleared out. When I tried to stop him, he hit me twice. So I hit him back. Once," Nick said firmly.

Both men looked between Nick and Willy.

"Is this true?" Gary asked.

"Yeah, I hit him. Only because he snuck up behind me. I was just taking the horses out for exercise," Willy said.

"Wilbert told him to say that if you arrived," Nick said dryly. He'd overheard his uncle prepping Willy. "I have really good hearing," he told his uncle, whose face grew red with anger. "They honestly thought they could clear out the barn before I returned," Nick added. "Until my father's will is read, this is still my property."

"According to who?" Wilbert asked.

"The law," Nick replied. "I was in the room when Stephen McKinney told you so," he pointed out.

"He's right," Kyle said. He turned to Nick. "Do you want to press charges?"

Nick thought about all the mess and hassle that would cause. "No, but I don't want either of them stepping foot on my land again," he said firmly. "Not until after the will is read."

Kyle and Gary turned towards Wilbert and Willy.

Then Kyle said, "That's a nice new truck you got there, both of you." He motioned to the new truck with the trailer and to the one Wilbert had driven up in. Nick hadn't noticed it until Kyle pointed it out. Both trucks were brand new and had temporary stickers on them. "Must be nice to be able to afford something like that." Kyle walked over to Wilbert's truck.

Wilbert's smile doubled. "Sure is. We just picked these up this morning. I even got the missus a new SUV." Wilbert was always one to brag.

Nick instantly wondered how the man could afford three new cars. He worked a part-time job down at the local warehouse while Willy worked at the lumber yard.

Gary whistled and leaned against his patrol car. "I looked at one just last month. How much did each of those set you back?"

Wilbert's eyes flashed over to Nick quickly and, suddenly, Nick got a sinking feeling.

"Didn't cost nothing. Yet," Wilbert responded as his chest puffed out.

"Yet?" Kyle asked. "How'd you manage that?"

Nick took a step closer to his uncle as his hands balled into fists.

"Dad's lawyer said we could put this place up as collateral, since everyone in town knows the ranch is rightly his," Willy blurted out. Wilbert glared at his son.

"You..." Nick started, but his anger was too great to allow him to continue.

"Bucky gave me these here trucks and Marge's SUV because he knows I'm gonna get this place in the end," Wilbert said firmly. "When everything is transferred into my name, I'll have plenty to pay him off. All this will be mine finally."

Bucky's was the local car dealer that sat just outside of town. His was the only car dealership for about a hundred miles of Cedar. He was also one of Wilbert's best friends.

"Now, that there is fraud. You don't own this place. Not yet," Kyle said smoothly. "Putting up property that isn't yours legally is a crime." He moved towards Wilbert.

"Not according to..." Willy started, but Wilbert jerked his head towards his son.

"Shut up, Willy," Wilbert shouted.

"Wilbert, is this true?" Gary asked. "Did you purchase these trucks by putting this ranch up as collateral?"

"I ain't saying nothing until I talk to my lawyer," Wilbert barked out. "Come on, Willy, let's go home."

The three of them watched Willy and Wilbert climb into their new trucks and drive off. Willy took a little longer since he had to back up the truck and the trailer before hauling out of the driveway fast.

"If I were you, I would've pressed charges," Kyle said under his breath as he headed back to the patrol car.

"Give us a call if they come snooping around again. Until your father's will is read, I'd stick close to the property. I wouldn't put it past those two to try something else," Gary added.

Nick watched the patrol car disappear down the driveway and cursed under his breath. He put the horses away and then called Stephen McKinney and relayed everything that had just happened.

"As executor of the estate until your father's will is read, I can assure you, neither Wilbert nor Willy has any right to put the property up as collateral. You don't even have that right at this point. As I mentioned in our meeting yesterday, your father put me in charge of everything financial until after the reading. His only stipulation was that you remained on the property until then. He left no previsions for Wilbert or his family. I'll have to make a few calls to clarify things. I'll start with a call to Bucky."

"Yeah, I figure that's a good place to start too," Nick agreed.

"Are you okay?" Stephen asked.

"Yeah," he answered as he wiggled his jaw. "Just pissed. I don't know why my dad decided to play games like this. Is there any way we can speed up the reading?"

"No, all I can say is your father had his reasons," Stephen said. "I'll keep you posted what I find out."

After hanging up with Stephen, Nick headed inside and up the stairs to the room he'd moved back into when his father had gotten sick. His little cabin that sat on the back of the property sat empty now. Most of his things were still in the cabin, but he figured he would move it all over after the will was read. Either that, or he'd be packing it up to move off the property.

Glancing into the mirror, he groaned at the sight of his swollen lip and eye. He was covered in hay and sweat and decided what he needed was a long hot shower.

When he stepped out, he felt a little steadier and more refreshed and not as frustrated as before, especially after reading the text message from Stephen.

"Talked to Bucky. Wilbert presented him with a deed to the ranch, which is why he opened a line of credit for the three vehicles. I'm having him email a copy of what Wilbert gave him. Whatever it is, it is fake. I assure you, the deed has not yet been taken out of your father's name. I'll keep you posted.–S"

Heading down to his father's office, he decided to meet

with Daryl and the rest of the workers later that day. He sent Daryl a message requesting he gather everyone at the barn in an hour for the meeting. Currently, there were eight people working on the ranch, not including Daryl, four of which were camping out on the property.

For the next hour, he tried to make heads and tails of his father's office. His mother had been the tidy one in the relationship.

There were scraps of paper, notes, messages, and receipts all over the desk. By the time he walked outside, he had most of it in organized piles.

All eight of the employees were standing around chatting when he stepped outside. Their chatter stopped when they noticed him.

"Good afternoon. Thanks for carving out a few minutes of your workday," Nick said, stepping beside Daryl.

"Wow, are you okay, boss?" Daryl asked, motioning to his face.

Nick touched his lip and winced. "Yeah, I got this the same way you got yours." He motioned to Daryl's eye. "Which is why I've called this meeting. Until further notice, neither my uncle Wilbert nor my cousin Willy are allowed anywhere on this property. According to the law, until my father's will has been read, I am in charge of the ranch along with my father's lawyer, Stephen McKinney. I know there are rumors going around..." At this point, several people mumbled, and Nick held up his hands to stop them. "Let me assure you, they are just rumors. I don't know my father's intent for pushing the reading out for so long, but I'll do what I always have done. I'll follow his wishes. Until then, we run the ranch like we did under him. Nothing changes. Got that?" He waited until everyone nodded. "Good. Now, if you see either my uncle or cousin on the property, feel free to call the police or me. Do not try to approach them yourself." He motioned to Daryl and then himself. "They haven't stopped at physical violence yet, and I wouldn't put it past them to step up their game." He waited a beat. "Thanks, that's all for now."

Everyone turned and disappeared except Daryl.

"We were just about to take the east heard out to pasture. Want to ride with us?"

Nick thought about how relaxing the hour-long ride would be, but then remembered he needed to stick close to the property just in case his uncle or cousin came back. "No, thanks. I want to, but... I'd better stick close to the house."

"Gotcha." Daryl nodded. "If you need us..."

"Thanks." Nick nodded and watched three of the men jump on the horses already saddled up. With the exception of Thunder, Lightning, Bolt, and Crash, there were half a dozen other work horses that were kept at the barn near the ranch houses.

Daryl and the hands were in charge of caring for those animals. Occasionally, they would need a new horse or a trip to the vet.

Every month a farrier would come out and shoe all the horses that needed attention, and their vet, Dr. Roselyn Stein, would check on all of their animals. Dr. Rose, as Nick had always called her, was one of the nicest people in Cedar. The woman knew everyone and every animal.

She came around more often in the spring when it was calving season. After the crew left, he saw Dr. Rose drive up and park just outside the barn.

"Hey, Dr. Rose." He smiled at the older woman, then noticed the younger woman with her.

"Nick." Dr. Rose smiled as she shut her door. "This is my granddaughter, Emma. Emma, Nick Howe."

"Nice to meet you," he said. Emma was roughly his age. He turned to Dr. Rose. "You're far too young to have a granddaughter."

Dr. Rose's smile grew. "Flatterer. Just like your father." Dr. Rose waved him off. "Emma is going to be shadowing me. Someday, she'll take over my practice."

"Well, then, welcome." He waved them towards the barn. "Let me know if you need anything. Dr. Rose pretty much knows her way around the place."

"Thanks." Emma smiled as her eyes ran over him.

Dr. Rose was already heading inside the barn with her bag and hadn't seen the interest in her granddaughter's eyes.

"Maybe we could hang out sometime? You could show me around town?" Emma practically purred.

She was cute, and normally he would have enjoyed flirting with her, but images and thoughts of Kara kept filling his mind instead.

"Thanks, but I'm... pretty busy." He turned when he heard Kara's truck heading up the driveway. She parked next to his truck and got out, her eyes going between him and Emma.

"I saw the police cars earlier. I would have come then but I was out riding and then Bella got spooked and dumped me in the stream," Kara said, her eyes still going between the two of them. "Who's this?"

"This is Emma, Dr. Rose's granddaughter," Nick said. "Emma, Kara Montgomery. She lives just..." He motioned to Kara's place.

"Oh, right, we're going to be heading there later this week," Emma said. Just then her grandmother called her into the barn. “It was nice meeting you,” Emma said to Kara. “Later,” she said to Nick.

Kara stopped beside him. “She likes you.” She nudged his shoulder.

He glanced over at her, and she gasped. “What happened to your face?” She took his face in her hands and scanned it. “Who did this to you?”

“Who else.” He moaned.

“Your lip is bleeding.” She dabbed it with her fingers.

He touched the spot with his tongue. “Yup.”

“Come inside, I’ll clean you up.” Kara practically dragged him into the house. Instantly, his mind went to her dragging him other places and what he would do to her. How he would please her. How she would please him.

CHAPTER ELEVEN

Nick was very quiet as she cleaned him up. She asked him what had happened and after several short sentences, she figured the rest of the story out. She surmised that he didn't want to say much since she was cleaning up his bloody lip.

But when she was done, he sat there on the edge of the countertop just looking at her.

"What are you doing here?" he finally asked.

"I told you. I saw the police cruiser," she answered, feeling stupid. She'd been so concerned, she'd pushed Bella into heading that way. The horse hadn't wanted to cross the creek and that was how Kara had ended up soaking wet. She'd had to return home, shower, and change before she could come over and see what had happened.

Thankfully, at that time, the trucks and police cruiser had disappeared.

"You could have called or texted me," he pointed out.

"My phone is sitting in a bag of rice," she explained. "It ended up in the creek with me."

He smiled slightly. "You really did end up in the creek?"

She chuckled. "Yes, although at the time, I wasn't laughing about it. It was freezing." She rubbed her hands together, remembering how cold the ride back to the barn was. "Poor Bella, I left her in the stall without brushing her. She didn't end up in the water, just standing over me looking as if I deserved it." She smiled.

"She'll survive," he said, taking her hands in his. Then he pulled her close. Before she had time to respond, he was kissing her, her body plastered against his, their mouths fused as his hands roamed over her.

"After the day I've had," he said between kisses, "I just needed a little sunshine."

She held onto him and felt the tension release even more.

"Stay for dinner?" he said next to her skin.

She nodded, unwilling to let him go. It felt too good to be next to him.

"This time, I'll cook for you," she said against his lips.

"We can cook something together." He straightened up, then took her hand and led her through the house to the kitchen. "I didn't thaw anything, so we'll have to figure something out."

After a few minutes debating, they came up with the idea to do chicken parmesan.

While she oversaw the noodles and the salad, he worked on the chicken and the sauce.

Instead of sitting in the formal dining room like they had a week before, they sat in the smaller nook area off the kitchen. Here, the back windows overlooked the land beyond. She could just make out the creek that crossed over both of their properties. The one she'd fallen in earlier. The one they had first met at all those years ago.

Remembering how that first meeting had ended up with Nick on his ass in the mud, she laughed out loud.

"What?" he asked, frowning at her.

"I was just remembering the first time we met." She smiled and watched him grin.

"Before we put up the fence that clearly shows we were on my property," Nick added.

She narrowed her eyes. "The tree is still on our property."

He raised his eyebrows slightly. "The tree may be, but the rock on which you were sitting on that day isn't."

"Let's agree to disagree," she said with a laugh.

"Agreed." He held up his beer, and she tapped her bottle to his. When their eyes locked, he sobered. "I don't want things to change between us."

"They won't," she reassured him, not sure if it was true.

"I mean it. You've been here for a long time. Even if..." He sighed. "I can't be around."

"Don't say that. Your father wouldn't do that to you." She took his hand in hers.

His eyes were glued to their joined fingers. "Kara, that's not what I mean." His eyes moved up to hers. "After the kiss... I don't want things to change between us," he said again.

She felt her entire world shift slightly at the thought of not being friends with Nick. She wondered if something as strong as heartbreak could wipe away all the years of friendship. She wasn't sure it would be worth it.

Instead of answering, she nodded and swallowed her fears.

After they finished the meal, they stood in the kitchen

and did the dishes together. The sun had already gone down, and she knew that it was time to go home. But something kept playing over in her mind. The desire to have him touch her started to bubble deep in her gut and spread throughout her entire body.

As if he could read her mind, he finished drying his hands and then took her hips and pulled her close, wedging her between his body and the countertop.

"Kara?" he said, his eyes glued to her lips.

"Hm?" She watched his mouth move and wished more than anything that it would cover hers soon.

"Stay." His one word had her knees weakening. To answer him, she lifted on her toes and placed her lips over his. When the kiss grew heavier, he hoisted her up on the countertop. She wrapped her legs around his hips and pulled him closer to her.

Feeling his hardness pressed against her core, every fiber in her body lit on fire. She wanted, needed, more than she ever had before.

Her fingers dove into his hair, holding him to her as she poured everything she was feeling into the kiss. Trying to prove to him, to show him, just how much she wanted him.

"Kara," Nick groaned against her lips.

"I need..." She ended on a moan when his hands snaked under her shirt and cupped her breasts.

When she reached for him, however, he pulled back. His eyes locked with hers as he started removing her boots. He moved slowly, as if he had all the time in the world. Didn't he know she was on fire? Couldn't he see it in her eyes?

When her boots hit the floor, their eyes locked as he reached for the zipper of her jeans. Her shirt followed and landed in the pile of her clothes. As she reached for his, he yanked off his shirt, and she was momentarily frozen in place as her eyes ran over him while he toed off his shoes and removed his jeans.

When they were standing in the kitchen in nothing but their underwear, her in an amber silk set and him in black boxers, it was as if the air itself crackled around them.

"You're sure?" he asked softly.

To answer him, she rushed towards him and placed her mouth over his. He hoisted her up in his arms, and she wrapped her legs around his hips again. He took a few steps backwards until she was once more sitting on the edge of the countertop. Her hands roamed over his arms, his chest, every part of him that she could while he did the same to her.

Her bra was tossed aside moments later after his fingertips brushed underneath, playing with her nipples. When she was free, his mouth covered each nipple as he took it into his mouth and ran his tongue over her heated skin.

She almost lost it right there, and he hadn't even really touched her. While his mouth played over her, his hands cupped her hips. With each breath, she willed him to feel her. To pull her panties aside and dive into her heat. She was impossibly hot and wet, waiting for him.

When his hands finally did cup her silk panties, she moaned, and his mouth returned to hers.

"I want to take you upstairs," he said against her mouth. "I need to." He wrapped his arms around her.

She wanted to tell him no. To stay here. To take her right here, but he was already carrying her towards the stairs. She held onto him as the anticipation built even more.

The staircase was made of thick wood beams. There

was a small loft at the top, with two hallways leading in different directions.

Since her eyes were focused only on him, she didn't see where he'd taken her. Nor did she care. When he laid her down on a bed, she shifted and tried to pull him down with her. He briefly disappeared to grab a condom from the nightstand and then reappeared above her.

His hands roamed over her again, this time with a little more urgency while she nudged his boxers from his hips. He shifted to lay beside her as he continued kissing her.

As she wrapped her fingers around him, he nudged her panties aside and slid his fingers into her.

"Nick, I need you," she practically begged.

"Soon," he promised as his mouth traveled down her neck while his fingers slid in and out of her slowly. "Let me enjoy you for a moment."

He shifted and slid her panties down her legs, then knelt above her as his eyes ran over her entire body.

Since she was enjoying the view of him, she didn't mind.

He had glorious muscles all over thanks to all the hours of manual labor on the ranch. She wanted to take her time and explore each and every one, but she could feel herself building and knew that if he touched her again, she'd explode.

Then his mouth covered her between her legs, and she screamed as her entire world exploded with her release.

When he returned to cover her, her hands gripped his hips as he slowly trailed his mouth over her neck.

"Nick, don't make me beg," she said, and when she heard his chuckle, she dug her nails into his hips. Then, in one quick move, he slid into her, and she knew there wouldn't be any going back to how things were before.

Their friendship was officially over and the fear of losing it along with him weighed heavily on her as their bodies cooled later.

"I'd better get back home. Oliver probably needs out," she said, feeling a pain in her chest.

Nick shifted until he was looking down at her. "Nothing has changed," he said, before kissing her. "I still want you."

She nodded, holding back the tears. "Yes." She tried to smile and was thankful it was too dark for him to see her face clearly.

He seemed to understand her need to retreat and rolled from her. By the time she sat up, he was there with a T-shirt for her to slip on.

"Here, you can wear this. Our clothes are still downstairs," he said with a smile.

"Thanks." She pulled on his shirt and was surrounded by his sexy scent. She instantly wanted to keep wearing it when she left.

She followed him downstairs and slipped on her jeans and boots while he pulled on his own jeans and the shirt that he'd tossed off.

She tucked her shirt under her arm along with her bra and socks.

When she turned, Nick was watching her. Then he moved over and kissed her.

"I'll be over at your place in the morning," he said softly against her lips.

She wanted to argue. To tell him he didn't have to bother. That she could take care of the place by herself. But the truth was, she wanted to see him again.

"Okay. Thanks for dinner," she said as he walked her to the front door. "Wow, it's really coming down now," she said after they opened the door. “I thought we were going to have at least a week without snow.”

“Yeah, we’re supposed to have about a week of this stuff.” He stopped her from walking to her truck by pulling her close again. “What are you doing for Christmas? I mean, with your folks gone and all.”

“I’m not sure. My stepbrother and his family spend Christmas in Hawaii.” She shrugged. “I know my folks are going to be in Paris and plan on celebrating with a trip to the Eiffel Tower. I was thinking about going over to Liz’s place and spending it with her and her family.” She frowned. “What are you doing now that...” She felt her heart sink.

“I’m not sure.”

“We could... spend it together?”

He smiled. “I don’t want to ruin your plans with Liz.”

“I haven’t officially made any,” she admitted.

He sighed and then pulled her close and kissed her until she melted against him. “Kara, go home,” he said against her neck before he pulled away.

On very unstable legs, she walked through the snow to her truck, drove home, and then let herself into the house, where Oliver was waiting at the back door to be let out.

She was too wired to go to bed and decided to make banana nut bread for breakfast instead. Halfway through preparations, however, the energy she’d had melted and instead of baking the bread that night, she put the mix into the fridge for the morning.

She headed into her room, showered, and pulled on the warmest pajamas she had before crawling into bed.

Seeing the text message from Nick when she pulled her phone out of the bag of rice had her smiling.

"Hope your phone works again and that you got tucked into bed okay. Miss you already."

As Oliver jumped up on the end of her bed and did circles to get comfortable, she texted him back.

"Yes, phone is okay. Me and Olly are all snuggled in. You?"

"I've got Lenny and Squiggy in bed with me. Wish you were here too."

"Same."

There was a long pause before his next reply.

"Assure me that we're not moving too fast. We have known each other for over thirteen years."

"No, we're not moving fast." She snuggled further into bed. "Goodnight, Nick. See you in the morning."

"Night. Dream of me. I know I'll be dreaming of you."

CHAPTER TWELVE

Early the next morning as Nick was getting ready to walk out the door and head to Kara's place, the phone rang, and he ended up having a half-hour conversation with Stephen McKinney. The lawyer had an update on the paperwork that Wilbert had given the dealership to get the loans for the three vehicles.

The document was an obvious fake. Stephen had assured him again that the deed to the ranch was still in Nick's father's name. He'd even emailed him copies of both. The one that his uncle had given to the dealership didn't even have a state seal on it.

His uncle was getting sloppy trying to get his hands on the place. Which meant that he and his cousin wouldn't hesitate to keep trying.

When Nick stepped outside, he had to answer a few questions from Daryl and a few of the other employees. Most of them would be spending the day checking the fence lines and repairing parts of the hay barn, which was in serious need of repairs.

Nick had talked to his father last spring about

rebuilding it, but his father's health had taken first priority and the task had been put off for another season.

It was almost lunchtime by the time he parked beside Kara's truck and got out. Oliver was napping on the front porch, lying in the sunlight, and when he stepped up to pet the dog, he realized there were some really good smells coming from the open front door.

"Come on in," Kara called before he had a chance to knock on the door.

"Something smells good in here," he said as he and the dog stepped inside.

"I started making banana bread last night and when I woke up, I had the urge to bake even more," Kara said from the kitchen. She had flour on her shirt and on the tip of her nose.

He walked over and pulled her into his arms and kissed her. He instantly felt better.

"There, I've been thinking about doing that since you left last night." He pulled back.

"Is something wrong?" she asked, pulling back to run her eyes over him.

"No." He smiled. "Just a busy morning."

"More problems?" she asked as she turned back to mixing something in a bowl.

"No." He leaned against the counter and watched her. "Is any of that for me?" He motioned to the covered containers sitting on the stove.

She smiled. "That depends." She walked over and uncovered a pan. "Do want banana bread or pumpkin bread?"

He felt his stomach growl. "Can I have both?"

She laughed. "Yes, sit." She motioned to the table. "I'll get you a plate."

He walked over and took a seat. She set a plate of bread in front of him, a dollop of melting butter on each, along with a cup of coffee, which made him realize that he hadn't even had a cup that morning. No wonder he was in a bad mood.

Sipping the coffee and digging into the bread, he felt a little steadier and glanced up to watch her slide a pan of cinnamon rolls into the oven.

"Tell me I get one of those when they come out." He felt his stomach growl even more at the thought of it.

She laughed. "If you're still hungry, you can have as many as you want." She turned the blender on to mix the frosting.

He liked watching her bake. Liked that she seemed to enjoy it as much as he enjoyed working in the kitchen himself.

When she finally sat down across from him with her own plate of buttered bread, she looked happier than she had since her parents had left.

"Things are going well?" he asked her between bites.

"I love baking," she said with a sigh.

"Why don't you do it more often?"

She shrugged and her smile slipped. "There's never really that much time to."

"This bread is better than anything I can buy in town," he said truthfully.

Her eyebrows rose slightly. "Thanks."

He reached across the table and took her hand in his. "It's the truth. Have you thought about selling it?"

She frowned. "Selling? Like you're selling your jelly?"

"Amongst other things. I made enough last year at the local farmers markets and in a few hand-selected stores to buy my truck."

She sat up, and her eyes got a little wider. "Seriously?" She bit her bottom lip.

"You could always try. The next farmers market is this Sunday. I'll bet since it's the week before Christmas, you'd make a killing. Some people don't like to bake for themselves for the holidays. Especially if they're traveling. If you made a dozen of each of these"—he motioned to the breads —"a bunch of those"—he pointed to the oven—"along with a dozen or so pies, I'd wager you will sell every last one."

She tilted her head. "I could sell some of the cinnamon rolls and coffee cake along with slices of bread individually. You know, for people to eat as they're walking around."

"Throw in some Christmas cookies, and I'd bet you'd make a killing," he said, taking another bite.

She bit her lip again. "I don't know if I have time to..."

"Hey, remember, you have me to help out around here. Use me."

She smiled and then laughed. "Okay, I won't turn away free labor. Not when I could possibly earn enough to buy a new truck. Or at least new tires for mine."

For the rest of the morning, while they enjoyed the cinnamon rolls and worked around the ranch, they talked about what would be needed for her to sell her baked goods at the next farmers market.

Normally, he had Cheryl, the wife of one of his workers, man the booth at the market. He gave her a small cut of the profits. She also sold some of her jewelry in the booth.

He called her and she agreed to letting Kara set up another table with her baked goods this weekend.

Kara decided she'd need a full day to prepare, which meant he'd have to make sure everything ran smoothly at his place. She'd called Liz and her best friend had agreed to help her bake and prepare everything.

Since his father's death, he'd realized that even with his dad's failing health, the old man had done more than he'd known.

His phone rang constantly that morning while he helped Kara. Shortly after lunch, he had to leave her and head back to his place to deal with a broken flatbed truck, which they used to haul the hay out to the fields. Then there was a small fight between two temporary workers. In the end, he had to let the instigator go, and he and Daryl escorted the man off the property.

It wasn't the first time that had happened, nor, he figured, would it be the last. Part-time workers were hard to come by, especially in Wyoming.

His full-time workers were steady enough that Nick didn't have to worry much about them. Thankfully, by the next day, the worker had been replaced with another.

Still, it was almost noon by the time he made his way over to Kara's place. He found her in the barn, trying to clean some riding gear.

"Sorry I'm late," he said, stepping inside the barn.

She glanced up and smiled. "You're not. Remember, you're only helping me out. You don't work here."

He took her hips in his hands and then pulled her into a kiss. "It's been crazy the last few days. But I just want you to know, I really want to see you again." He brushed his lips across hers.

He felt her relax in his arms as the kiss deepened. "I'd like that," she said when he pulled back.

"Tonight?" he asked, then winced. "Scratch that. Tomorrow night?"

"Can't tomorrow. It's Liz's birthday. She wanted to head into town and go dancing."

"I can dance," he said with a smile. "If you let me know

where and when you're going, I can just happen to bump into you?"

She laughed. "Where else is there to dance in Cedar? The Firehouse."

He kissed her again. "How will Liz take it if I crash her party?"

She shrugged. "I think it depends on what you bring her or how many drinks you buy."

He laughed. "What is she in the market for?"

"A man, but she can't have you," Kara said, pulling him back down for another kiss.

From there, she had him run out and refill all the water troughs. He spent a few minutes with Wilbur before hunting Kara down in the hen house.

She was trying to hammer a board onto the roof of the house, but she wasn't quite tall enough to reach.

"Here," he said, taking the hammer from her and easily pounding the nail in.

"I could have..." she started, but he glanced down at her and she shut her mouth. She pouted up at him. "I could have done it myself."

"You needed a ladder. You're too short." He started hammering another nail in. "This hen house needs rebuilding."

"Yes, I know. I've told my father..." She let out a large sigh. "Dad was going to do it when he got back. This will help. Thanks."

He smiled, knowing it took all her willpower to say those words.

"Anytime," he said after he was done. "Anything else I can help with?" He looked around.

She followed his gaze. "No, not today. It's supposed to

snow again tonight. I wanted to go for a ride, but..." She shook her head.

"How about a short walk then?" he suggested, needing the fresh air and time with her.

She smiled. "Sure." She set down the rag she'd wiped her hands on. He took her hand, and they headed out across the yard.

In front of the home there was a large oak tree, the kind most would hang a swing from. All of its leaves were long gone, making it a twisted dark figure that they headed towards.

"I can't wait until spring," she said with a sigh.

He chuckled. "We just started winter."

She rolled her eyes at him. "Three months ago. Besides, in the last week we've had enough snow for a full winter. Christmas is next week. We are definitely in the middle of winter."

"Right, but we'll get snow for the next five months. Don't you enjoy the snow?"

"I love the snow, but in the spring, this tree blooms with the most beautiful pink flowers." She motioned to a smaller tree that sat next to the oak. "In the fall, its leaves are the first to change to a bright red." She lifted her face to the sky and took a deep breath. "Winter is fine if it's snowing. If it's not, it's just..."

"Depressing," he finished for her, understanding. Each day since his father's death, he'd slipped deeper and deeper. When the snow came or when he was with her, his spirits lifted.

Stopping just under the tree, he pulled her into his arms.

"This is good?" He needed to hear it from her. Wanted

to make sure she wasn't having second thoughts about him. It had been days since they'd been together. Too many days.

Kara smiled and he relaxed. "Yes, this is good." She lifted onto her toes and kissed him. "Which surprises me, and I think surprises you too."

He shrugged. "I had a clue it would be."

She nudged his shoulder, then her smile slipped a little as she looked over her shoulder. "There's a truck outside of your place." She motioned.

He glanced over and groaned. "Shit." He dropped his arms and started heading towards his truck at top speed while he pulled out his phone to call Daryl.

Kara was on his heels. "What can I do?" she asked just as Daryl picked up.

"It's okay, boss," Daryl said. "It's Bucky."

"I'll be there soon." He hung up. "It's Bucky. Not my uncle." His pace slowed.

"What do you need?" she asked when they reached his truck.

He pulled her into his arms and kissed her until they both relaxed into one another. "You," he answered. "Just you."

"Tomorrow at the Firehouse. I'll plan on you driving me home," she said with a smile, then she pushed him towards his truck.

"Kara?" he said, getting in the truck.

"Yeah?"

"I plan on waking up with you the following morning." When she nodded, he shut the door and headed back to his place.

Sure enough, Bucky was standing on his front porch when he parked next to the new truck.

Bucky—no one knew or remembered what the man's

last name was... maybe Bucky *was* his last name—was a Cedar staple. He was one of the largest business owners in the area, which earned him instant respect.

However, since Bucky was close to Nick's uncle, he was always cautious around the man. Nick and his father had always traveled to Casper for any of their vehicle needs.

"Nice day," Bucky said when Nick stopped beside him.

"Sure is," Nick answered and then motioned to the truck. "Looks like you changed your mind about working with my uncle."

Bucky nodded and then slapped Nick's shoulder. "It's your problem now."

"Mine?" Nick shook his head as Bucky started walking towards another waiting truck. "I never signed a loan with you."

Bucky stopped and looked at him. "Your ranch was put up as collateral for this truck and the other two vehicles. When I get them back from Wilbert, they'll be delivered here. My office will be in contact about payments—"

"Like hell," Nick broke in as he pulled out his phone and called his lawyer. "Stephen, I've got Bucky here trying to unload those three vehicles my uncle tried to purchase with the fake deed."

"What?" Stephen answered, then groaned. "Shit. I'll be right over. Don't say or sign anything."

When Stephen showed up half an hour later, Bucky was fuming. Nick had sat down on the porch after telling the man he was not taking possession of anything and waited without a word while Bucky paced and cursed.

"Someone's gonna pay for these," Bucky shouted at Stephen. "I special ordered these all the way from Denver for Wilbert."

"And Wilbert is currently sitting in the county jail for fraud."

"Wait," Nick broke in. "If you special ordered these and my uncle took possession of them the day after my father's funeral... When did he order these?"

Bucky frowned. "The beginning of November."

"Long before my father was even in the hospital?" he asked, and Bucky nodded. Nick growled and stormed towards the front door. "I'm expecting you to handle this," he said to Stephen and then slammed the door behind him while he went inside to call his aunt and get more details.

If this was true, his uncle had been planning this for a while. Which just pissed Nick off even more.

CHAPTER THIRTEEN

The next night, Kara and Liz walked into the Firehouse and within minutes had drinks in their hands as they headed to the dance floor.

Liz had come over early with several outfit choices and had settled on a black top that pushed up her ample Ds, a tight black skirt, and her red cowboy boots, which she said were lucky. Kara wore a white bustier with her jean skirt and her black cowboy boots. Even though Kara's Cs were no comparison, the bustier showcased them well enough that the moment they had stepped inside, she had caught several men staring. Most likely they were looking at Liz, but Kara didn't mind. Nick had promised to meet them there.

Sure enough, less than half an hour later, Nick waved to her from across the dance floor. Since her drink was empty, she made her way towards him and watched his eyes heat when he noticed what she was wearing. He had on a dark gray T-shirt, jeans, and his boots and hat. He looked every part the cowboy.

"Hey, cowboy," she said, leaning against him. "Want to dance?"

"Wow," he said, running his eyes over her face. "Just wow."

She stepped back and did a little twirl for him. "You like?"

"That outfit should be illegal," Nick said, pulling her back into his arms and kissing her.

"That kiss should be illegal in public," Liz said from beside them, causing them both to laugh. "I need a drink." Her friends' eyes narrowed on Nick. "You're buying. I want a burger and fries too." She pointed at him and walked over to take a seat in a booth.

Kara laughed and then shrugged towards Nick. "It's the price you have to pay for crashing tonight."

He kissed her again. "One I'm willing to pay. Go, sit down. I'll order. Burger?"

"And fries and another one of these." She held up her beer. He took the empty bottle and made his way towards the counter while she went over and sat next to Liz.

"He's got it bad for you," Liz said.

"What makes you say that?" she asked, leaning on her friend.

"I recognize the look," Liz answered.

"Like you've ever seen the look before." She rolled her eyes. "When have you been in love?"

"Not me personally. But I have had plenty of men fall in love with me," Liz joked.

Kara laughed. "Like who?"

"Whom, and..." Liz glanced around the room and started pointing and naming off several of the men in the bar.

"That wasn't love," Kara said, just as someone sat at their table. Believing it was Nick, she smiled and glanced over. Her smile fell away instantly when she saw Willy sitting next to her.

"Well, well. We heard there was a party going on here tonight," Willy said as two of his buddies, Dean and Mike, sat in the empty spots.

Dean was built a lot like Willy—thick everywhere and not necessarily with muscles. Mike, however, was tall and thin and worked at the mill. Kara knew that the guy could lift bales of hay without even breaking a sweat. The three of them together would easily scare anyone they ganged up on.

"You're not invited, Willy," Liz said. Kara poked her friend in the ribs, trying to signal her not to egg the trio on. "What? It's my birthday. If I don't want to have to put up with their bullshit, I shouldn't have to," Liz replied.

Kara poked her again.

"Oh, well, it's your birthday? I guess I'll have to make sure and give you a big fat juicy present." His eyes ran over Liz's breasts, and he actually licked his lips. The other two laughed.

"Dream on, Willy," Liz said strongly. "The only thing big and fat you have is your head. And I wouldn't let you get near me if you were the last man on earth."

Kara stabbed her finger into her friend's ribs. "Shush," she hissed.

Willy wrapped his hands around Kara's arms, ready to yank her out of the booth to get to Liz, but a hand dropped on Willy's shoulder.

"Let her go," Nick said in a low voice.

Willy's smile grew, and Kara realized this was exactly what Willy had wanted.

"Nick," Kara warned, but Willy's fist was already in motion. She watched in horror as it connected with Nick's stomach. She was impressed when Nick didn't even wince.

He'd seen the punch coming and had stepped back far enough that Willy's fist only grazed his gut.

Willy didn't get a second swing before Nick yanked him off the bench. He landed on the floor facedown.

Dean and Mike started to get up, but a glance from Willy had them relaxing back.

"I got this," Willy hissed as he got up off the ground.

Just then, Kyle Morgan and his wife stepped over. Just seeing the officer, even out of uniform, had Willy straightening up.

"Is there a problem?" Kyle asked, his eyes glued to Willy.

"No sir," Willy sneered. "Just... fell out of the booth."

Kyle's eyes narrowed slightly. "I think you and your boys have had enough fun for one night. Don't you?" Kyle said firmly.

Willy's eyes narrowed slightly. Instead of answering, he motioned to his two friends, who slid out of the booth and followed Willy into the crowd.

"Liz, I heard it's your birthday," Kyle's wife, Emma, said. The woman had been one of Liz's and Kara's favorite teachers in high school. "Happy birthday, sweetie."

"Thanks, Mrs. Morgan."

"We'll leave you young kids to your party. My husband promised me a few dances before we have to take the babysitter back home," Emma said with a wink as she tugged her husband's hand and pulled him out onto the dance floor.

"Are you okay?" Nick asked, sitting across from them.

"Yeah," both she and Liz answered at the same time.

"What an ass," Liz said, taking the drink from the waitress when she set a tray down on their table.

"The food will be a few more minutes," the waitress said and then disappeared.

"He was obviously trying to get to me," Nick said with a sigh. "His dad is sitting in a jail cell, waiting for his court date on Monday."

"He's in jail?" Liz asked. She took a sip of her beer.

"They arrested him yesterday on fraud. He made a fake deed to the ranch and tried to pass it off as real to put up for some pretty big purchase like the new vehicles and a few other items around town," Nick said. "He honestly believed that once he took over the ranch, he'd get everything, all the money and the bigger income."

"What will happen to you if they get your ranch?" Liz asked.

Kara took a sip of her beer and tried not to think about that possibility. She loved her place. Really. But the thought of living next to Willy scared her.

Nick glanced at her briefly before answering. "I'd maybe travel for a while."

Her heart skipped at the thought of traveling the world with Nick for a year or two.

"I've always wanted to go to Italy," Liz said. While they ate their food, they talked about where each of them would like to travel and what they had hoped to see and do in other places.

After she was done eating, she pulled Nick onto the dance floor. Over the years, she'd seen him dance. He'd taken loads of girls to the Firehouse, and she'd watched and wished from afar.

The man knew how to move. Feeling him up against her tight as they bumped to the fast music was a different kind of thrill that she'd never experienced with any of her previous partners. Liz was beside them, dancing with one of her exes. The man looked completely gone over her. Liz looked like she was just having fun.

Then the music turned slow, and her desire bubbled deep within her, almost causing her to pull Nick into a dark corner.

"How much more of this are you going to torture me with?" he growled into her ear.

She wanted to leave with him. To have him drive them back to her place and...

She caught sight of Willy and his goons cornering Liz. The trio had her blocked in the back hallway near the bathrooms. Her blood went cold when she realized they were pulling Liz out the back door. She had never seen that look of sheer panic in her friend's eyes before.

She pushed away from Nick and rushed across the dance floor and out the back door before it even closed. She used all that anger and pushed Willy off her friend. She caught him off guard and, once more, Willy ended up on the floor, this time on his ass.

"Stay away from my friend," she yelled as she reached for Liz. But she wasn't quick enough, and Willy jumped up and wrapped his hands around her neck. Then he yanked her off her feet and shoved her against the outside brick wall of the Firehouse.

She heard shouting as the back of her head connected with the wall. Her feet dangled in the air as stars exploded behind her eyes. Everything swirled and then tilted several times while she was held, shoved, pushed, and eventually, released.

She coughed a few times when Willy's hands were removed from her throat. She'd fallen to the sticky ground of the alleyway, bent over on her hands and knees as she tried to draw a breath.

"Kara!" Liz was shouting her name.

She wanted to respond, but her throat had closed up and she just couldn't get enough air.

"Help!" Liz shouted. "Someone help her."

She heard more shouting and felt someone push past her. The back door was opened as more people rushed out. She shivered at the thought of what would have happened if the three men had taken Liz away.

"I'm here, Kara." Nick's voice caused her to focus and calm. "I'm right here. Breathe," he said, and finally she calmed enough to suck in a deep breath.

"I... I'm okay," she croaked out. She coughed a few more times. Her hands covered the spot where Willy's had held her against the wall.

She was lifted and carried back into the warmth of the building. When she was set down, she realized that the music had completely stopped. The entire room was quiet and as she opened her eyes, she noticed that the house lights were on.

Liz was sitting next to her, holding her hand, looking very worried.

"Are you okay?" Liz asked.

Kara nodded and swallowed, then winced at the pain.

"Here," their waitress said, handing her a bag of ice. "This might help." She handed one to Nick. "Here's one for you too, hero."

Kara glanced over and saw the blood dripping from Nick's lip. His eye was swollen again but he was watching her closely.

"Gosh, look," Liz said when Kara moved her hands away from her throat. "He tried to kill you." Her friend touched her neck softly. "You're purple here." Liz held the ice to Kara's throat, and she winced. She wanted the warmth instead but knew the ice would prevent swelling and leaned back.

Her eyes met Nick's, and she could tell he was worried for her just as much as she was for him.

"What happened?" Kara asked, feeling a little fuzzy.

"Nick kicked all three of those assholes' butts," Liz explained. "Willy took off like the rat that he is. They were boasting about how they were going to take me out and show me a real good time for my birthday," Liz said quietly. "I think they..." Her friend's voice hitched.

Kara set the ice pack down and wrapped her arms around her friend.

"I don't know what I would have done if..." Her friend cried.

"That's it. Tomorrow, I'm buying you some mace for your birthday. Maybe a taser." She closed her eyes tightly.

Liz sighed. "Okay. Just as long as you get some too."

Kara nodded.

"I'll buy," Nick piped in. "I know just the place to get it all. But first, we're having you checked out," Nick said as two paramedics came into the room.

After everyone was checked out and patched up, the three of them walked out to Nick's truck. It was decided that Nick would drive Liz home, since neither of them wanted to take their eyes off Liz until they both knew she was home safe.

"Sorry your celebration got cut short," Nick said as he parked behind Liz's parents' car in the driveway.

"Thank you for being there. I'm not sure what we would have done..." Liz dropped off as she wrapped her arms around Kara with the seat between them.

Her best friend still lived above the garage behind her

childhood home, and her parents were both standing on the porch as she got out and rushed to them.

"I should have been watching out for her better," Kara admitted when she watched Liz's parents hold onto her friend.

Nick reached over and took her hand in his and squeezed it lightly. "We both should have been on better lookout. Liz is strong. She's got her family to comfort her. The police have Mike and Dean in custody and are looking for Willy."

"What does it matter? They technically just fought back after I attacked them," Kara admitted. Kyle had informed them once things had settled down that there wasn't much the three could be charged with. It wasn't like Willy's father being charged for fraud. A bar fight and the potential kidnapping charges were all hearsay. Only Nick had seen Willy choking her and, even now, the redness was a faint pink. And there wasn't any evidence the three men planned to hurt Liz. They were claiming Liz went with them willingly. It was their word against hers and Liz's.

"It's a start," Nick said as he pulled out of Liz's driveway and headed towards their places.

She shivered and wrapped her arms around herself as they drove out of town towards their homes.

When they reached her driveway, she felt steadier and under control. Nick had talked to her the entire drive, keeping her mind from what could have been.

He shut off his truck and turned to her. "Feeling better?" he asked in the darkness of the cab.

"Yes," she sighed. She unhooked her seatbelt and slid over to him. "Thank you for keeping my mind occupied." She dipped her fingers into his hair and pulled his face towards hers.

"Anytime," he said against her lips. "I didn't want to mention it earlier, but you were pretty impressive back there. From what I saw. The way you jump tackled Willy." She heard him chuckle. "You looked like you were wrangling a steer instead of a two-hundred-pound overgrown man-child."

She laughed. "That's exactly what he is, and it felt like it. I could have torn his eyes out for the way he made Liz afraid."

"You know, I never really liked Liz, before tonight. I mean, I always thought she was the empty-headed cheerleader type," he admitted, causing her to laugh even more. "What?"

"Oh, she'd love to hear you say that. She worked hard to get that reputation after they found out in fifth grade she had a higher IQ than anyone else in the county. Her parents wanted to pull her out and put her into college instead of sixth grade."

"She's that smart?" Nick asked.

"Let's just say she had to try hard to not let anyone else know that her brain is bigger than her cup size," Kara joked. "She single-handedly made sure I passed algebra and French."

"Why didn't she go away to college?" he asked as they walked into her house.

Kara frowned. "Liz has... some phobias. Some pretty bad ones. She's decided it is best she stick around home. She took a bunch of online classes and ended up getting several degrees. That she does absolutely nothing with," she finished as she unlocked the door. "She loves running her place. She claims she was born to run a business. Even a hair salon." She smiled. "She loves hair as much as running a business."

She shut the door to the house behind them and pushed Nick against the wall.

"Now, enough about my friend." She ran her hands over his chest and arms as his hands moved to her hips.

"Okay." He smiled at her. "What do you want to talk about instead?"

"Absolutely nothing." She went on her toes and kissed him and then pulled his shirt over his head.

CHAPTER FOURTEEN

Nick's mind went completely blank when Kara pressed her body against his. The different ranges of emotions he'd gone through that evening made it feel like his heart was on the end of a yoyo. He'd been pulled from being turned on dancing with Kara to fear and anger mixed with worry, and now he was back to being so turned on that it physically hurt him.

When his shoulders hit the wall and Kara's hands started removing his clothes, it took him a couple of seconds to rein in his desire. Then her fingers wrapped around him and everything that had been building for her was released in a wave of passion.

He reversed their positions, pinning her against the wall as his hands snaked up her legs, under her skirt. He pushed her panties aside and buried his fingers into her heat. He marveled in the welcome he felt there. She was so hot, so wet, and his cock jerked in response as he slid his fingers in and out of her.

Her soft moans were making him even harder for her,

making him move differently, just to get more of those sexy sounds from her.

She reached for the zipper of his jeans as he hiked up her skirt. Then he lifted her, and her legs wrapped around his hips. Seconds later, he thrust into her, causing them both to moan.

He listened as her breath hitched with each of his thrusts. Her nails scraped his shoulders, his arms, trying to pull him closer, to hold on to the moment.

"Don't hold back," he said into her hair as he felt his control slipping.

"Nick," she cried out as he felt her convulse around him, causing him to release his own hold and follow her.

"Are we really lying naked on the entry floor?" Kara said sometime later.

He chuckled and continued to run his fingertips over her hip.

"Is that a problem?"

She shook her head as her eyes met his. "Not yet, not until I start feeling again and realize just how hard and cold this floor is."

He'd already noticed it. His hip was sore from the wood floor and there was a breeze coming in from under the front door that he was blocking with his body so that she didn't feel it. Then he realized that a dog was whining and glanced over to see Oliver sitting at the back door.

"Olly needs out," Kara said as she reached for her shirt.

"I'll let him out." He quickly got up to pull on his jeans. He stood by the back door as the dog did his business. When he returned, Kara was dressed again and looking through the fridge.

"Hungry?" she asked over her shoulder.

"I could eat. Are there any of those cinnamon rolls left?" he asked, feeling his stomach growl.

"You read my mind." She pulled out the pan. "I'll heat them up first."

While they waited, she pulled out her phone and sent Liz a text message.

"How is she?" he asked after he heard a response come in.

"Good. She's resting. Her mother responded." Kara set her phone down. "Willy has always been a jerk, but tonight, he and the others took it a step too far."

"They'd bragged back in high school about all sorts of things. No one ever paid it any attention though," Nick admitted. "Now I feel like a jerk for not taking the rumors more seriously."

"Rumors?" Kara asked.

He shrugged. "About hurting animals or beating up other kids. All three of them bragged about who they had slept with." He narrowed his eyes. "At one point, they all three bragged about you."

"Me?" Kara's eyes grew big. "They bragged about sleeping with me?"

He nodded. "No one, and I do mean no one, believed them. Not when you made it very clear what you thought of all three of them. Especially Willy." He smiled.

"Yeah, I wouldn't. Even if he was the last man on earth," she said firmly.

He smiled and took her hand in his. "I think everyone in town knows that."

"Good. But they crossed the line tonight. Which is why I pressed charges against them. Why I convinced Liz to as well."

"Smart move. I just wish it would help more. I'd wager

the two of them will be out by morning and since Willy took off, I'll bet his lawyer will clear him of anything before they can even slap cuffs on him."

"I just don't get how your uncle and cousin still have so much pull in this town. I mean, everyone knows they're crooks," she said with a sigh.

Nick shrugged. "Wilbert has spread the story of that he was cheated out of the ranch and his inheritance around town for years. I guess a lot of people believe he's the underdog and root for him no matter what."

The timer went off on the microwave, and she stood up and gathered their plates.

"Let's take these into my room," she suggested. "We can watch something and fall asleep."

They sat in her bed and watched a movie while eating the sweets. Olly curled up at their feet on the bed. Then he held onto her while she fell asleep in his arms.

He'd never spent the night with anyone before and wanted to enjoy every minute of feeling her body next to his while he drifted off.

When he woke, he realized there were other benefits to the arrangement. Kara was so warm and soft and plastered against his body. His arm, which had cushioned her neck all night, was asleep, but she was making the rest of his body feel too good for him to notice.

As he opened his eyes, he ran his gaze over her face. She'd taken a few minutes to wash the makeup from her face and pull on a sexy tank top and matching shorts to sleep in in. Her face was even more beautiful clear of product.

He willed her to open her eyes so that he could get lost in the deepness of their blue. But her dark lashes remained closed. Her lips were too inviting and as he brushed his mouth across them, tasting them, he felt her shift in his hold.

"Mmm," she moaned against his lips. Her body shifted until they were chest to chest. He could feel her puckered nipples through the silk, against his bare chest.

His free hand snaked under the tank top, cupped her breasts, then he used his fingertips to pinch the peaks gently. Her entire body arched into his, rubbed against his.

Again, he felt the immense desire. He was powerless to fight what he felt for her. He nudged the shorts down her hips, then he cupped her, slid a finger, then two, inside her, parting her legs with his knee. She rolled over and lay flat on the bed while he slid his fingers in and out of her slowly.

"Oh god," she said against his mouth. "Please."

Her hips moved with his motion as he watched her face, watched the pleasure cause her cheeks to flush. She sucked her bottom lip into her mouth, held it there between her teeth as tiny soft moans escaped.

His eyes roamed over her body, over her peaked nipples he could clearly see through the soft tank top. Down her flat belly, her exposed belly button, to where his hand moved slowly in and out of her. He watched his fingers slide in, disappear into her, and come out slick.

He could smell the sexy perfume she'd worn the night before, her shampoo, the fabric softener on the sheets, her sex.

The desire to taste her had him shifting over her. His hand continued to move as he licked his way down the same path his eyes had just taken. He paused and sucked each nipple through the material, wetting it, causing her skin to peek even more through the silk. He dipped the tip of his tongue into her belly button, rolled around it, before moving lower to where his fingers disappeared inside her.

Finding her clit, he licked and then sucked lightly until her hips bounded off the mattress and her fingers dove into his hair while she cried out his name.

He shifted above her again and watched those blue eyes of hers go wide as he slipped into her, fully embedding himself until he held firm and lowered his mouth to her ear.

"I love the look of you, the taste of you," he said softly as he remained still inside her. "I love the feel of you wrapped around me." He kissed her neck softly as her legs wrapped around his hips. "I love you," he said as he started to move inside her.

He wanted to ignore how she had stiffened when he'd admitted his feelings to her. Wanted to, but after they had both been pleased, she disappeared into the bathroom and he'd gotten a phone call from Daryl, telling him he should return to the ranch immediately.

"Kara?" He knocked on the bathroom door.

"Yes?" she replied without opening the door.

"There's some sort of emergency at the ranch. I need to go," he said, wishing she'd open the door.

"Oh, okay. I could—" she started, and he heard her moving around.

"No, stay. I'll..." He felt stupid. He shouldn't have told her. Not like that. Not after everything that had happened last night. He should have planned for candlelight and flowers. Not bruises and police reports. "I'll talk to you in a bit."

"Okay," she said through the door.

He gathered his things, finding his socks and shoes by the front door. When he drove up to the house, he could see instantly what the problem was. Every piece of furniture on the wide front porch had been cut to pieces with the axe that normally sat in a log on the side of the house. Some of it had just been tossed into the yard. The planters his mother had always filled in the spring with brightly colored flowers were in pieces all over the yard. He'd continued the tradition of filling them with plants every year since her death.

Even the sign that hung above the front doors, which he and his father had made years ago, had been yanked down and snapped in two.

Daryl was standing on the steps waiting for him.

"Have you been inside yet?" he asked Daryl.

"No." He sighed. "Too bad you had me keep Lenny and Squiggy down at my place last night. They might have scared off whoever did this."

"Willy," he said, unlocking the door. "This was Willy." He groaned as he stepped inside.

"I've called the police," Daryl said, stopping just inside the door.

The inside matched the outside. Most of the furniture was broken. Mirrors, glass vases, picture frames, and small tables.

Nick made his way through the house and noticed the back door torn completely off its hinges.

"I guess this will teach me about staying away," he said softly as he kicked a pan that lay on the floor.

As he made his way through the house, he realized just how pissed Willy must have been to destroy so much. Not a single room was left untouched.

Most of the special items his mother had set around the house were destroyed. All of the small feminine touches that he and his father had left after her passing were now gone. And it really pissed him off.

By the time the police arrived, he'd checked every single room. All but the guest room upstairs had been gone through. Willy hadn't bothered with clothes or closets or thankfully the pantry full of rows and rows of glass jars. But he'd smashed every single mirror. Every single picture frame was destroyed. All of the dishes lay in pieces in a pile in both the kitchen and the formal dining room.

The end tables and chairs were nothing more than kindling now. There wasn't a lamp left in the entire house. Some had even been thrown out upstairs windows, smashing the double-paned glass and frames.

Kyle and Gary walked through all of the rooms with him, then informed him that he'd have to make a list and take pictures of all of the destruction. He knew he would have to do that anyway for his insurance company, thanks to a phone call to Stephen.

He signed a police report, then shot off a copy of it to Stephen as the cruiser pulled out of the drive. He watched as Kara's truck stopped at the entrance while she chatted with Kyle for a moment.

Then her truck flew up the driveway, and she rushed to hug him on the porch.

"Kyle told me. I'm so sorry," she said into his chest.

"It's just things. They can be replaced," he said, more for his benefit than hers.

She leaned back and cupped his face. "Most of it was your parents' memories." Tears rolled down her cheeks. "What can I do to help?"

He thought of telling her he could handle it, but he realized he wanted her around. Even if she didn't return his feelings. Yet. He was a patient man. For something as good as she was, he figured he could wait a very long time for.

CHAPTER FIFTEEN

It took them two entire days to clean up his house. On the third day, she had to get ready for the farmers market but knew that he would make the rounds at her farm to feed and water the animals as he promised.

It ate at her that she hadn't gotten a chance to talk to him about... what he'd told her the night of Liz's birthday.

She'd wanted to return the words, but her fear had stopped her. Fear that she had never said those words to anyone before. Did she feel the same for him that he felt for her? Could it just be lust?

In the end, she had kept her mouth shut and helped him haul out every broken item. He'd burned the broken pieces of furniture. The rest had been hauled to the dump by Daryl or one of his workers.

Since there wasn't any proof that it was Willy that broke in, all the police could do was visit him and give him a warning. Even his father was released the following day to await his trial, which was rumored to take place sometime after the holidays.

She knew Nick was determined not to give either of

them another chance at his place, so there wouldn't be a repeat of the other night anytime soon. Which was a complete shame.

She wished more than anything to wake up each day like she had that morning next to Nick.

Even as she and Liz spent the day in the kitchen baking, preparing everything for the farmers market, her mind replayed that night and morning she'd spent with him.

Liz had, thankfully, stepped up big time. Not only had her friend helped her bake, but she had also spent the night for much-needed friend time. Liz agreed to help her at the market the following day as well since the salon was closed on Sundays.

Even as they packed up everything for the market, she continued to dwell on her feelings about Nick's confession.

Did she love Nick?

She didn't have the answer to that question. Not yet. Sure, she loved being around him. He'd pretty much been there her entire life, at least the part that she could remember. He'd been an enemy to begin with. He'd shifted to a friend sometime much later. Then, he'd been... well, competition after her parents' left for their vacation. Now, he was an interest in other ways she wanted to keep exploring.

She enjoyed his company. Enjoyed the sex. Liked his humor. His work ethic. Not to mention the way he filled out his jeans. And all those pretty muscles he let her play with each time he took his clothes off.

"Earth to Kara?" Liz snapped her fingers an inch from her nose.

"I'm here," she said, rolling her eyes.

"I think we have everything," Liz repeated, glancing around the kitchen.

Kara had been baking since two that morning and was on about her sixth cup of coffee.

"The market starts in an hour. We'd better head into town if we plan on having all of this set up by then." Liz waved her hands at all the containers of pies, breads, cookies, and rolls she'd made.

"Right." She took one more glance around and then locked the door behind them.

"So, do I get a cut of today's profits?" Liz asked as Kara drove into town.

"I think you ate your share of profits this morning," Kara joked.

"Hey, no one would blame me. Those cinnamon rolls are delish." Liz glanced back to the back seat.

"No, you can't have another one," Kara said dryly, causing Liz to groan and cross her arms over her chest in a pout Kara knew all too well. "You can have some cookies after you've finished helping me set everything up."

Liz smiled. "Deal."

It took them a little while to find the booth that Cheryl had set up near the pavilion in the center of town. The middle-aged woman was one of the biggest health fitness gurus in town. She ran her own yoga studio out of her garage on the weekends and made jewelry when not homeschooling her three young children.

Both Kara and Liz had purchased many items from her in the past few years. Not once, however, had either of them known that Florence's Jams was actually Nick's business.

Cheryl had already set up all of the jelly and jams but there were two large tables empty just for her baked goods. Liz had brought a display case that they ended up putting the individually wrapped cookies and cinnamon rolls in.

Before they were done setting up, she'd sold three

cinnamon rolls. It was repeatedly suggested that the coffee cart be moved to sit beside them next time.

An hour after the market opened, Nick strolled over. He looked tired but happy to see her.

She knew from texting him that he'd spent all night repairing the upstairs windows that had been busted out.

"Morning," he said, wrapping his arms around her. When he just held on and took a deep breath in her hair, she smiled.

"I get the idea you need some sugar to get you going." She nodded to Liz, who took out a cinnamon roll for Nick.

"I can run and get us some coffee," Liz suggested.

"I'd kiss you, if my heart didn't already belong to Kara," Nick said with a sigh.

Kara's heart did a little flutter just hearing those words. She couldn't tell if it was a good flutter or the kind you got right before stepping on a carnival ride that looked dangerous but was still fun.

Liz smiled as she handed him the cinnamon roll. Then her friend took everyone's coffee orders, wiggled her eyebrows at Kara, and disappeared.

After that, she stayed busy and didn't have a chance to talk to Nick again. When Liz returned, Kara's coffee went untouched until it was cold, thanks to all the people stopping by the booth.

The farmers market usually ended at one o'clock, but by noon she was completely sold out. She had a few custom orders for the next market.

"How much did you make?" Liz asked as she took out the last cookie she'd stolen before someone else stopped by to purchase it.

"I haven't counted it yet. A lot of people paid me on my app." She motioned to her phone. "I've made over two hundred dollars just in app deposits today. Not to mention the cash and checks." She tapped the money bag that she held to her chest. "Which I'm going to deposit first thing in the morning."

"If you're going to continue selling at the market, you should create a business. You now, get a license, a bank account. The whole works," Liz suggested. Then her friend snapped her fingers. "You should open a bakery."

Kara laughed. "Right."

"What? There isn't one in Cedar. Not after Sunrise was closed. The place next to mine is empty and my parents own the building. I could talk to them." Liz motioned to her parents, who were standing at the base of the Christmas tree, talking to the mayor.

Kara shrugged, not wanting to admit to her friend how wonderful that sounded. It was far too early to dream about anything other than getting through another farmers market.

The truth was, she loved her ranch and enjoyed working with the animals just as much as she loved baking. But she was beginning to wonder if she wanted to be tied to doing it each day. There was so much to do around the place. Especially with her parents gone.

"Wow, you sold out?" Nick said when he came back to the booth. He'd wandered off at one point and, seeing the bundle of flowers in his hands, she realized he'd gone off to purchase them. "For you," he said, handing them to her. "Congratulations on being a huge success. You're the most exciting thing to hit this market in a while. Everyone's been talking about how wonderful your cookies are."

Kara buried her face in the bundle of wildflowers and took a deep breath. They smelled like spring, even as the crisp cold air blew over her face.

"Of course they love her baking," Liz said. "She's amazing. Maybe you can convince her to open up a bakery. I think I can speak for everyone in town when I say there is no way I'm waiting another month to get my sugar fix from these." She shoved the last bite of a cookie into her mouth.

"That's a good idea. I was just talking to Tom about them opening a coffee place. He's signed a lease on the old gas station building across the street." He motioned to an old fifties-style gas station that had at one time been converted to a historical diner. A few years ago, when the economy tanked in Cedar, the place had been closed down and had sat empty ever since.

The old pumps still sat there, unused, but the entire front of the building had been blocked off and made into a patio sitting area.

Liz's salon sat opposite that and the empty place next to it would be perfect for a bakery. People could walk from the coffee shop to purchase baked goods. "They're planning on opening up after the New Year," Nick finished.

Kara bit her bottom lip as she thought about providing baked goods to sell on a daily basis. Could she do it? Did she want to?

Kara's heart did that stupid little skip again, and this time she knew it matched how she felt right before stepping onto a very scary ride. Still, there was enough excitement there that she promised to think about it.

As Nick was helping them gather their things to haul to Kara's truck, a loud bang rang out feet from them. The loud pop echoed in the grassy area. At first, Kara thought it was the sound of thunder, but then Nick tackled her to the ground. Liz screamed and fell beside them as two more shots rang out.

People screamed. People ran. People hid.

Then everything went silent as everyone looked around for any sign of who was shooting.

Police sirens caused Kara's ears to ring, and she gently nudged Nick as several police officers rushed past them.

"Are you okay?" Nick asked.

"I'm okay," Kara told him after quickly assessing herself. "Liz?" She looked over to her friend who was staring at her with a confused look.

Then she noticed blood trickling from Liz's arm and rushed over to her friend.

"Help! She's been shot!" Kara cried out. She gripped her friend's arm, applying pressure as blood oozed between her fingers.

"Here," Nick said. He ripped the tablecloth she'd just folded up and applied a torniquet just above the wound. "We need an ambulance," he said to Cheryl.

"Over here!" Cheryl called out as several more officers rushed by. "Someone's been shot."

"Over here!" someone else called out a few feet away from them. "Help!"

Kara couldn't tear her eyes from her friend's pale face.

"Don't you dare die on me," she said to her friend. "I refuse to go into business without your help," she said as tears flooded her eyes, blocking her vision.

"Kara," Liz said softly, her voice sounding a million miles away.

"She's in shock," Nick said as Kara was pushed aside. Her shirt and hands were soaked in her best friend's blood. They loaded Liz onto a gurney and rushed her towards a waiting ambulance. She followed them, as Nick held her upright.

"I'll drive us to the hospital," Nick said, steering her

towards his truck. He helped her inside, and she watched as if in a daze as they followed the ambulance.

"Oh god," she cried as the realization that her best friend has been shot hit her.

"Hey," Nick said, taking her bloody hand in his equally blood-soaked hand. "She's going to be okay. It looked like the bullet just grazed her. I think she was in shock more than anything."

"Yes." She closed her eyes and tried to remember everything she could about her friend's arm.

The bullet had torn apart Liz's jacket. Nick had torn the rest of the sleeve off and then... Kara knew Nick was right. There had been a lot of blood, but from what Kara had seen, there had just been a long, deep gash in her friend's upper arm just under her shoulder.

There was no way the bullet could have hit anything major. Right? Muscle. Most of that area was muscle. Right?

She reached up and touched her own shoulder, using her fingers to explore the same area.

"It's all muscle here, right?" she asked Nick, who glanced over at her. His eyes moved to where she was touching before nodding and returning his eyes to the road.

"Yeah. If I remember correctly from health classes, it shouldn't have hit anything major." That made Kara relax a little.

"Okay, so... maybe she'll have some stitches. Maybe some muscle damage," she said, more to reassure herself than anything.

She closed her eyes again, then they flew open. "I have to call her parents." She fumbled for her phone.

"Kara, they were there. They're in the ambulance with Liz. That's why you couldn't ride with her."

"They were?" Kara frowned.

"I think you were sort of in shock too," Nick said, touching her arm. "It looks like you're back under control."

"I... I'm sorry." She took a deep breath.

"Don't be. She's your best friend. We just went through something really crazy."

"I don't know what I would do without her. She's the only reason I'm still in Cedar," she said as tears rolled down her cheeks. "I love it here, but without Liz..." She shut her eyes on the fear.

She'd been so involved in her own pain that she didn't notice what her admission did to Nick. She didn't see the pain or the hurt that crossed his eyes. But when she opened her eyes and looked deep into his, she realized that there was a new reason she wanted to stay in Cedar. One that meant as much to her as anything else. Maybe even more. But it was still too early to admit that to herself or anyone else.

CHAPTER SIXTEEN

It was strange being back at the hospital. Even though he knew that this trip wouldn't end in as much sorrow and loss as the last time, it still stung.

They rushed into the emergency room and waited with Liz's parents for an hour before they were told that Liz was okay. Her parents were shown back to a private room where Liz was recovering just fine.

Liz had been very lucky and had only received ten stitches. She'd also apparently hit her head on the edge of the table when she'd fallen. The doctor seemed more worried about that than the bullet graze.

While they'd waited, they'd overheard that two more people had been shot. One of them was an out-of-town guest who had been shot in the leg and was expected to make it.

The other was Rudy, a kid they'd gone to school with. The nerdy kid who had always kept to himself had been shot in the heart and died on the scene, feet away from his brother and mother.

The police believed the shooting was random and had

no suspects yet. They were asking anyone with video or photos of the day to send them to the police station's email address for review.

While they waited to see Liz, they both scrolled through their phones and sent what they could.

"Liz took more photos than I did today. She even did a video of me. I was too busy selling stuff to bother," Kara admitted as she scrolled through her phone.

They had gone to the bathroom after they had arrived and washed most of the blood from their hands and clothes. Still, he could see some dried blood under her fingernails.

It reminded him how close they had been to losing one another. That thought had him holding onto her a little tighter as they waited.

When Kara was told she could go back and see her friend, he waited alone and thought about his future. With or without her.

She hadn't returned his feelings yet, at least not verbally. He knew that didn't necessarily mean that she didn't love him. After all, when they were together, she showed him that she did, even if she didn't know it.

So how could he get her to realize just how much she meant to him? The flowers had been just the start. He figured he didn't have much time to show her, to prove to her, just how much better they would be together than apart.

Three hours later, he drove her back to her truck. Cheryl had finished loading all of Kara's things into the back of it. She'd found the bag of money Kara had made on the ground and held onto it until she could give it to her in person. She'd also found Liz's cell phone and had delivered it to Liz's family at the hospital after everything settled down.

Nick followed Kara home and texted Daryl to ask him to check up on his place, as he wouldn't be home until later that night.

When he walked into her house behind her, Daryl's text response came in. He read it quickly.

"Is everything okay?" Kara asked.

"Yes, Daryl says everything is quiet at home. He let the dogs out and is taking them for a walk." He set his phone down and wrapped his arms around her.

"Who do you think it was?" Kara asked against his chest.

It was the first time she'd asked it, but not the first time he'd wondered the same thing.

"Do you think it was Willy or any of his gang?" she asked, breaking into his thoughts.

He couldn't say it out loud, but it had been all he'd been thinking since hearing the first shot ring out.

He'd believed they had been coming after them—Liz, him, and Kara—in retaliation for the other night.

The question of why the shooting had been wild weighed on him though. Had they intended it that way? Had they been drunk? High? Or were they just bad shots?

He knew the three men dabbled in drugs and had been drunk or drinking almost every time he'd had a run-in with them.

He was sure that the police were looking into the three. Especially after what had happened to Liz on her birthday.

It wasn't as if Cedar was crawling with criminals. Besides Willy and his gang, there were a handful of high school students causing issues in town. A group of them had been caught breaking into the school but the problem was mostly vandalism.

This didn't smell of a bunch of high school kids pulling

a prank. This was direct. Whoever had shot at the market had intended to hurt and kill.

"I don't know," he finally said. "They would be the most logical guess. If I were in charge, I'd definitely look there first." He wrapped his arms more tightly around her. "Why don't you and Oliver come stay at my place tonight?" he suggested. "We can make some dinner, watch a movie?"

She rested her forehead against his shoulder. "I... need some time alone." She glanced up at him. "I promised Liz I'd be there tomorrow morning when they release her."

He nodded, feeling his heart sink a little. "Okay. I can still make you something to eat while you go clean up?" he suggested.

Kara took his face in her hands. "Nick, thanks, but... I'm too tired. I'm going to shower and then lie down." She lifted on her toes and brushed her lips across his. "I... thanks." She turned away from him.

Driving away from her place and going home alone was the hardest thing he'd had to do that day. Still, he figured he'd get some work done after making a handful of calls to determine what in the living hell had gone on.

After the first two calls, he turned on his television and watched the news replay some very grainy video. He instantly spotted himself and Kara helping Liz after the shooting.

Kara's face was pale as she shouted for help. The video zoomed in on him when he ripped the tablecloth and applied the tourniquet on Liz's arm. The reporter called him a local hero, but his eyes weren't on him or Kara. His eyes were scanning the background, trying to find any sign of the shooter or shooters, as the news hinted at.

The report ended with information that there were no

suspects in custody and that the police were looking at a few leads. He hit mute and went back to making his calls.

Kyle didn't take his call.

Gary did.

"I know why you're calling. No, we don't have any leads. Yes, we've talked to Willy and his gang. They've all vouched for one another. They claim they left the market half an hour before the shooting and were back at Mike's place. We're trying to confirm that," Gary said before Nick could even say a word.

"Was it one shooter or more?" he asked. "They sounded different. Like they were from different guns."

Gary was quiet. "We're checking on that."

"Did you also check on any guns Willy and the others might own?"

Gary was quiet again. "I can't discuss..."

"Damn it." Nick slammed his fist on the table. "What about the other night? What those three tried to pull with Liz? What's going to happen with that?"

"The three of them claimed they just wanted to give Liz a birthday gift they had for her out in Willy's truck. We can't charge them without proof a crime was actually committed. Since they are claiming that Kara attacked Willy to begin with, we can't do much about it."

After getting off the phone with Gary, Nick felt more frustrated and had even more questions than before.

He walked over to the kitchen window and looked out over to Kara's place. All of her lights were out now. He could just make out the dark building through the lightly falling snow.

Glancing down at the dogs, he motioned towards the back door and grabbed his coat, needing the fresh air to think.

Watching his father's dogs skip and play in the snow, he felt a wave of loneliness hit him. It was funny, he'd never thought about how lonely the place was before. Never had he imagined being there without his father.

Sure, maybe when he was an old man, but not before he'd turned twenty-five. Hell, what was he supposed to do with the rest of his life?

He turned back to his house, and seeing the place lit up with all the Christmas lights warmed him. He'd also left all the lights on in the kitchen and living room, making the place practically glow in the snow light. The place was massive. Too big for just him and two dogs.

His parents had always hoped to fill up the five bedrooms with children. They'd suffered multiple miscarriages after his birth. Then his mother's cancer had been discovered.

His eyes grew damp as he looked up at the home, but he laughed when Squiggy dropped a huge log in front of him.

"Want to play fetch?" he asked the dogs, who danced around his feet happily.

After a half hour of playing with the dogs, he headed back inside. He'd accidentally forgotten his cell phone inside and now saw many messages from Kara. He punched her phone number instead of reading each one.

"Hey," he said when she answered.

"Are you okay?" she asked, sounding worried.

"Yeah, I was just outside playing with the dogs. You?"

"We're on the news."

"Yeah, I saw." He glanced towards the still-muted television.

Kara was quiet for a moment. "Is... is it too late for us to head over there? I've just realized I don't really want to be alone. Not when whoever did this is still out there."

He smiled. "I'll come get you."

"No, I can drive. I'll need my truck for the morning trip to see Liz. We'll be over in a few minutes."

He stood in the kitchen, his eyes glued to her place. He watched as lights flickered on, then off. He saw her truck start and watched as it traveled all the way to him.

He was standing on the front porch with the dogs, waiting for her. Lenny and Squiggy liked Oliver, and they happily greeted the older dog, who walked into the house as if he owned the place.

Liz laughed. "Oliver thinks he owns the world."

Nick smiled and took her overnight bag from her hands. "Have you eaten?" he asked. She shook her head. "I was about to make some soup and grilled cheese sandwiches."

"I can help," she offered.

He set her bag at the base of the stairs and then wrapped his arms around her. "I'm glad you're here," he said into her hair. He could smell the fresh shower on her, and her hair was still a little damp.

He felt her shiver slightly as she held onto him.

"We got lucky today," she said against his chest.

"Yes, we did."

"Nick?"

"Hm?" He closed his eyes and tried to hold onto the moment.

"We can eat. After." She pulled back and looked into his eyes. "Take me upstairs. I need to feel alive. I need to be with you." She took his hand in hers.

Everything inside of him pulsed and slanted. Suddenly, his world shifted until its axis was here. Right before him. Whatever happened to him, or the ranch, no longer mattered. She was the center of his world. The center of his universe.

In one quick motion, he lifted her into his arms and carried her up the stairs. When he laid her down gently on the bed, he knew that this was his chance to show her exactly how he felt. Even if she didn't return the words, he had this chance to show her.

"Nick?" Kara said softly as he slowly removed her clothes. When he didn't respond, she took his face in her hands.

He could see what she wanted to say. Could see it there in her eyes. He didn't need the words. Didn't need to hear them. He got the feeling that she wasn't ready to admit to herself how she felt about him. So, not giving her a chance, he covered her mouth with his and showed her everything they could be together.

This time when the words slipped from his lips, Kara didn't jerk away or tense. Instead, she melted against him as he held onto her, as if they had to cram a lifetime together into one night.

CHAPTER SEVENTEEN

Waking up in Nick's arms was by far the best feeling in her life. This was the second time now they had spent the entire night in one another's arms. She hoped it wouldn't be the last, but every time he admitted his feelings to her and she didn't return the words, she grew more worried.

How long would it be before he grew discouraged and gave up on her?

It was true that the feelings she had for Nick were deeper than she'd had for anyone else. Of course, she'd only had a handful of boyfriends before now, and none of those relationships had lasted longer than a few months.

She and Nick hadn't even officially been an item longer than any of those relationships. Sure, they'd known one another longer than any of the other boys she'd dated. They had also been closer.

When her phone chimed, she rolled over and shut off the alarm as Nick's hands pulled her closer.

She laughed and then sighed when he rolled over her.

"Morning," he said after kissing her.

"Morning." She smiled up at him. "I need to—"

"Shower with me and eat breakfast before heading out to take care of your friend." He nodded. "I completely agree."

She laughed and tried to nudge him off, and he picked her up and carried her to the bathroom.

"There is only one way out of this house," he said, turning on the water and then setting her on her feet slowly. "Giving me what I want," he joked as he kissed her again. "You're better off. It'll be quicker," he said between kisses. "Or we could have our first fight?" He wiggled his eyebrows at her, causing her to laugh.

"We've had plenty of fights before," she pointed out as he started peeling off her clothes.

His smile widened. "Not since we've been an official couple."

"Is that what we are?" she said, starting to pull his shorts off.

His eyes met hers as his hands stilled. "Yes."

She saw the seriousness in his eyes and swallowed, wanting to change the subject.

As if he read her mind, he finished pulling off her clothes and stepped into the shower with her.

"The shower is too small for the both of us," she pointed out when the water hit her full force and missed him completely.

"Yeah," he said with a slight frown. "I've been avoiding moving my things downstairs into the main bedroom. Half my stuff is still out in the cabin. The bathroom downstairs is twice this size. I still have to purchase new furniture for down there as well. Most of it was busted in the break in."

"I can help you if you want. After I get Liz settled."

He pulled her close and shifted until the water hit him

in the back. "I'd like that. I have no idea how to decorate the place."

"We can drive into Casper after Christmas. The furniture stores usually have great deals after the holidays." She didn't want to tell him that she'd already made a few trips there to purchase gifts in the past few days.

He nodded, then leaned down and kissed her until they both forgot about anything except for one another.

While she dressed, applied her makeup, and dried her hair, Nick disappeared downstairs to make them breakfast.

When she stepped into the kitchen, he was just letting all three dogs inside. The kitchen smelled of bacon.

"I can keep Ollie here for a while," Nick suggested as they ate. "The boys like the company. I've got a few things to do around here, and then I'll take him home when I go check on your animals, if you want."

"Okay," she said as she took a sip of her coffee. She pushed her half empty plate aside. "I'd better get going."

"Be careful," he said, taking her hand. "I was going to call Kyle and get an update. Remember, whoever shot up the market is still out there."

She shivered at the thought of someone coming after him or Liz.

"I will," she promised. "I'm only going to the hospital and then to Liz's place."

He nodded. "Will I see you later?"

She thought about it and nodded. "I can come over again later tonight. You should just keep Ollie here."

He smiled. "Does that mean you'll spend Christmas with me?"

She wanted to tell him yes, but something had her shrugging instead. She had all his gifts over at her place.

"I'd better go." She got up, gathered her bag and coat, and left through the snow.

A few hours later, Liz was sitting against her headboard in her old bedroom in the main house as Kara sat at the foot of the bed reading the local newspaper to her. Christmas Eve was the following day, and the entire town continued to fixate on the shooting, even during all of the holiday celebrations.

"Does it really say that?" Liz asked.

Her friend's coloring was back to normal and, if Kara was honest, she looked perfect. Except for the white bandage on her upper arm, Liz was in perfect health. Thank god.

"It does." Kara showed Liz the newspaper.

Liz took it from her and laughed. "They're actually calling him a local hero?"

"Nick did rip the tablecloth in half and put a torniquet on you," Kara pointed out.

"I know, I've watched the video like a million times," Liz said with a smile. "A very sexy move. Who knew he had it in him?"

Kara wanted to say that she did but bit her lip instead.

"Gosh, you've got it bad for the guy." Liz laid the paper down in her lap.

"What?" Kara frowned.

Liz rolled her eyes and nudged her hip with her foot. "You're in love with Nick. If it's not obvious to you, it is to everyone else in town."

Kara swallowed and avoided her friend's eyes. "I..." She shook her head.

"Gosh, don't you dare cry on me," Liz warned. "It's not like you just got shot. You're in love. You should be happy."

"I..." She shook her head again, then sighed and rolled

her shoulders. Feeling the tension build, she stood up and walked over to the window and looked out at Liz's small snow-covered yard.

This was how she knew she belonged on a ranch and not in town. She needed the vastness and space. She hated seeing neighboring homes, even with all of their cheerful Christmas decorations and lights. The street out front was busy as three cars drove by. She wanted the hills. The fields of cattle. The open sky.

Closing her eyes, she finally admitted to her friend her fears.

"What if it doesn't work out?" she said, not turning around.

"Then it doesn't," Liz said casually. "Not everything does. But it's obvious to everyone else that he feels the same way about you."

Kara turned back around. "He's told me a couple times."

Liz smiled. "Then what's wrong?"

"I... I've never told anyone, any man, before," she admitted.

"There's always a first time," Liz said, shifting slightly.

"Have you told someone before?" she asked her friend.

"No, but someday when I do fall in love, I won't hold back. When you feel it, and know it's right, there's no use in wasting any time."

"I know you're right," Kara agreed. She knew she'd been hurting Nick by holding back her feelings. He deserved to be with someone who wasn't afraid of love. Wasn't afraid of saying so and showing it.

"Do you remember when we first met?" Liz interrupted her thoughts.

Kara smiled. "Sure, I was getting picked on by Willy

and his gang. It was my first day at school after moving here. You walked right up and took my hand and told Willy to shove it and sit on a tack. Then you pulled me away and we went to go play on the swings."

Liz smiled. "That day, I knew we'd be best friends. There was no doubt in my mind what I would feel for you." Liz held out her hand for Kara's. Kara walked over and took it, sitting next to her friend. "Kara, I love you. You're the most important person in my life beside my parents. I have never distrusted you or been afraid to show or tell you how I feel. What we have"—she held up their joined hands—"is real. And so is what you and Nick feel for each other. I can't say I'm not super jealous of it, but I can say that I'm not surprised by it either. You two deserve to be happy together. Don't waste a minute of it. You never know when someone with a gun will take that away. Rudy wasn't as lucky." Liz frowned. "He asked me out a couple times."

"He did?" Kara was shocked by this news. What she'd remembered of Rudy was that he was your average nerd. Smart. Thin. Usually spent more time indoors than out. He'd never been in any sports that Kara knew. Unless chess club counted.

"Yes. I didn't think he was my type, but in truth, we were both too smart for anyone else in town. Who knows..." Liz looked up to her. "I never gave him a chance. I should have."

Kara sighed and then nodded. "I know you're right."

Liz smiled. "Good." She nudged her shoulder. "Then what the heck are you doing here?"

Kara laughed, then leaned in and hugged her best friend. "I love you, too," she said as tears slipped from her eyes.

"Good. Now that you know you can say the words, go

tell the man who needs to hear them." Liz hugged her back and then pushed her away.

Kara stood up and then stopped. "How?" She turned back to Liz. "How do I?"

Liz smiled. "You'll find a way to make it what it needs to be. The most amazing moment of your life." She nodded, then pointed. "Go."

Kara laughed, gathered her things, and rushed out.

The entire time she drove home through the heavy snow, she thought about how to tell Nick how she felt. By the time she pulled up to her house, which was completely decorated with all the Christmas lights that Nick had helped her hang up, she'd come up with a perfect plan.

She rushed inside and grabbed the present she'd wrapped a few days ago from under the Christmas tree. She didn't need the box that held the sweater she'd purchased for Nick in town. What she needed was the big red bow that she'd used to hold the box together. She had plans to use it on his real gift.

With the bow in hand, she rushed out the back to the barn. She was so preoccupied with how to get what she needed for her plan to work that she hadn't registered the problem until she was halfway there. Then realization hit her like a brick to the back of the head.

Her entire body froze as her mind raced.

Now, as she held perfectly still just inside the barn doors, her ears ringing as she listened for sounds in the darkness, she knew in her bones something was off.

As with at the market, she completely froze for a full minute. Then she heard the sound of crackling grow loud and the smell of smoke hit her.

She gasped when she saw the flames coming from the top floor of the barn.

How had she not heard the sounds of the horses, the sounds of the rest of the animals crying for help? The noises they were making were deafening. Had the barn been on fire when she'd driven up? It had been so dark. She'd been so focused.

Without thinking, she rushed further into the barn to save as many animals as she could without another thought for her own safety. The big red ribbon fell to the ground and was quickly covered in ash and mud.

CHAPTER EIGHTEEN

Nick spent the first hours after Kara left doing his normal daily chores, letting the three dogs follow him around until Olly grew too tired and returned to lie on the back deck on the outdoor sofa. When he tried to let him inside, the dog rolled over and fell asleep, so he let him stick it out even though it was too cold for his liking. He made a point to check on Olly often while his dogs followed him around as if they were attached to him.

By noon, Olly wanted inside, but he was pretty sure it was because he was sharing his sandwich with all three of the dogs.

He received a call from Kara just as he finished up his lunch. She let him know that they had released Liz and she was heading out to have lunch with Liz and her parents before taking Liz back home. Kara wanted to help her friend get settled before coming back.

He assured her that he had everything under control and would be heading over to her place shortly. He had a few phone calls he wanted to make first.

His first call was to Kyle.

"I can't tell you much," Kyle said. "What I can say will be released to the press in about an hour. We found three different bullets. The one that struck Liz was from a .45. The one that hit the tourist was from a .22. The one that killed Rudy, was from a 9 mm. We've got a couple warrants to test a few guns. That's all I can tell you. I can't tell you who."

"Willy?" he asked.

"I can't tell you who," Kyle said and hung up.

His next call was to Stephen.

"Tell me my uncle is going to be locked up for good," he demanded.

"We're working on it," Stephen said.

"Damn it, can't you just let me know about my father's wishes?" he growled.

Stephen was silent. "Not until..." The man sighed heavily. "Your father's wishes are clear. I'm not allowed to read the will until certain criteria are met or until Christmas morning."

"Fine." Nick stood up and started pacing. "What happens if my uncle gets control of this place and then goes to jail?"

Stephen was quiet for a moment. "The property would default to his son."

"What happens if I gain control of the property, and something were to happen to me? Like... I get shot in the town square."

"The property would default to your uncle, unless you have a will in place that says differently," Stephen answered.

"Can I draw up a will without knowing the outcome of my father's will?" Nick asked.

"You can draw up a will anytime you want," Stephen answered.

"Then do it," Nick said.

"I'll draw it up after you answer a few standard questions. I can head out your way in about an hour for you to sign it. I'll bring a notary."

"Fine," he said and then answered all of his lawyer's questions as he paced the floor of his father's office.

After getting off the phone with Stephen, he left the dogs in the house and finished his errands around his property.

When Stephen and the notary showed up, he went over the paperwork and signed what he needed before heading over to check on Kara's animals.

He'd finished mucking out the stalls and had let most of the animals back into the barn. He was working with Wilbur when he heard a noise behind him.

Before he had a chance to spin around, something heavy hit him just behind his left ear, causing his world to go dark.

He woke in the darkness to the sound of screaming. The high-pitched sound pierced his ears and caused everything to spin as he threw up the lunch he'd eaten earlier. When his throat was clear, the smell of smoke suddenly hit him.

His vision was blurry as he reached around, trying to figure out where he was. The screaming continued and he realized it was Wilbur, the pig. His high-pitched squeals caused Nick's head to hurt so much, he had to cover his ears as he stumbled around in the darkness.

There was a wall of fire behind him and to one side, so he turned away from it and walked into the darkness of the smoke on the other side of the room.

The smoke had grown so thick, he couldn't tell where

he was. When he reached out, trying to find a wall, his hands came away from his head soaked with blood. He stared down at it as if it was the strangest thing he'd ever seen.

Then, suddenly, the squealing stopped, and he jerked his head in the direction he'd last heard it. "Wilbur?" he called out, wincing as the sound of his own voice caused his head to spin. The loud ringing in his ears drowned everything else out after that.

He moved slowly through the smoke and almost fell down the ladder that led up to the hay loft. When he noticed a pillar of smoke rising through the barn roof, he slowed down even further.

He was in the loft. How had he gotten up there?

He took each rung slowly, afraid he'd fall or the flames he'd just left would follow him.

When his feet hit the ground, he saw a dark figure standing just inside the barn doors. Smoke billowed around her as she held the reins to a spooked horse who was fighting her and standing on its back legs. Her jacket was wrapped around the horses' face, shielding its eyes from the smoke and flames. The horse had to trust and rely solely on its human.

Kara. Kara was risking her life for the animals.

Then Wilbur's loud squealing started up again. He was standing just outside the door of the pig's pen. He looked over and could just make out the large pig. He reached out and yanked open the gate. The pig didn't need any encouragement and bolted towards freedom, almost causing Nick to topple over.

He gripped the stall door across from Wilbur's pen and tried to steady himself. That's when Bella kicked at the door and nudged his head.

"Shit," he said, feeling sick again. He swallowed the bile and removed his shirt and tossed it over Bella's eyes. When he opened the door, the animal backed up into the stall. He took her harness and pulled as hard as he could, but he felt himself growing weaker while the horse kicked out and jerked backwards.

"Nick?" Kara rushed to his side.

"Bella." He motioned. "I've got her. Get out."

"We've got her." Kara took hold of the harness. Together, they pulled the animal outside.

When the horse was free of his T-shirt, she kicked and ran off through the field in the fenced area. Nick's knees hit the ground.

"Larry's still inside," Kara said.

Nick wrapped his hands around her ankles to stop her from going back inside.

"No, it's too far gone," he said, coughing.

"I can't." Kara shook her head and jerked free.

"Kara!" he called out and stood up to rush in after her. Everything spun and he fell to his knees again, dry heaving. "Damn it," he growled. He forced himself to stand up and head back into the now fully engulfed barn. "Kara!" he screamed over the sound of wood breaking and burning. There was a high-pitched hissing coming from the hay loft area that told him there wasn't much time.

He knew that at any moment, the entire second floor would come crashing down on them.

Then, something large flew past him, knocking him on his ass again. He coughed as he stood back up and covered his mouth with his hands. His eyes burned, his throat was on fire, and his vision was so dull, he couldn't make out anything.

"I've got you," Kara said, taking his hand in hers and

leading him further away from the barn.

When they collapsed in the snow and mud, he realized she'd had her shirt wrapped around her face the entire time. He lay in the muck, coughing and throwing up, as they watched the barn continue to burn.

He didn't know how long it took the firetrucks to get there. Or how long it was until the fire was out. He didn't even know if he'd passed out again or had thrown up anymore. For the next long while, his only memories were of coughing and blurry visions as shapes passed in front of him.

He couldn't even hear what people were saying through the loud ringing in his ears.

The one thing he did focus on was the feeling of Kara's hand in his through it all. He was lifted and then poked with something that made his body feel numb. He slept for a while and woke to the sound of Kara talking softly.

"Hey," he said, waking up quickly. "The horses?"

"All got out okay. Wilbur was a little singed, but the vet says he's going to make a full recovery. Daryl's put them all in your barn for now," she answered quickly.

"What were you thinking?" Kyle's voice sounded from somewhere across the room.

"About?" he asked, trying to get his eyes to focus on her or anything. He kept blinking, thinking they would correct themselves, but somehow, it only made his vision grow worse.

"Running into the barn in your state," Kyle answered.

"In... I was in the barn first. Someone hit me over the head and left me in the loft."

The room went quiet. "Did you see who hit you?" This came from Gary.

"No," he groaned. "Whoever it was must have been

strong enough to carry me up the ladder and drop me in the loft. Will someone tell me what's going on?" he asked.

"We've put out warrants for Dean, Mike, and Willy," Kyle answered.

"You think they did this?" he asked.

"We're not sure, but the three bullets I told you about yesterday, they match guns registered to the three of them."

"Yesterday?" He frowned.

Kara's hand squeezed his. "It's eight in the morning," she said softly. "You slept through the night."

He tried to shift and sit up. "The dogs?"

"Daryl has them," Kara answered.

"Okay, so the three of them decided to shoot up the farmer's market. Why?" he asked.

"To get to you is our guess," Stephen answered.

"Shit, my lawyer's here too?" he asked, trying to blink his eyes clear. "Why can't I see?"

"You've got a pretty bad concussion," Kara answered. "The doctor says your vision may be blurry for a few days and you may be dizzy as well."

"Did they think they could shoot me in the market?" he asked. "Why? To kill me to get their hands on the ranch?"

"My guess is payback. I guarantee they were drunk or high when they plotted it. So far, we haven't found any of them," Kyle said.

"Which is why you have a full police guard now," Gary added. "I was just relieving Kyle and filling him in."

"Gotcha." He leaned back and closed his eyes. "What does the doc say about food?"

"I'll tell the nurse you're hungry," Kara said as she got up and left the room.

"Nick." Stephen moved closer. "Your uncle was in the courthouse when I filled that paperwork yesterday. We estimate it was two hours after that when you were attacked and the barn was set fire to."

He tried to think back on how long it took him to muck out the stalls before he'd been hit over the head. "Yeah, sounds about right. Two maybe three hours." He nodded. "Do I have my phone? I could give you an exact time. I took a picture of Wilbur just before someone hit me over the head. The photo would be time stamped."

"Kara has it. We found it in the snow outside the barn."

Just then the door to the room opened again.

"Here, I brought some Jell-O for now and some water," Kara said.

"Do you have my phone?" he asked her.

"Yes," she said, and a moment later, it was placed in his hands. "I can't see a damn thing. Can you open my photos and let them know when the last photo of Wilbur was taken?"

The room grew quiet and then there was a combined gasp.

"What?" He sat up, almost dislodging the Jell-O she'd given him.

"There are two pictures here. Your phone must have gone off again when you got hit," Kara answered. "Nick, there's a picture of your uncle holding my dad's sledgehammer."

"We'll get another warrant," Kyle said dryly. "Send us a copy of that, would you?"

He heard Kara clicking his phone and then the whoosh of the photo being sent.

"What happens now?" Kara asked.

"Now, you two sit back and let us do our jobs. We'll keep a guard on your room until you're released," Gary said. "Or until your uncle and the others are picked up."

"Thanks." He held out his hand and a few seconds later, someone shook it.

"Get some rest, son," Kyle said. "I'll be right outside."

"Thanks," Kara added.

"I'll leave you two as well. I only came down to inform you that... Well, we can talk once you're home. Merry Christmas," Stephen said and then left.

"Damn, it's Christmas Eve." He sighed. "I... had the entire day planned out." He felt her hand slip into his again.

"Oh?" she asked. "Tell me what you had planned."

"They aren't by any chance going to let me out of here today, are they?" he asked instead.

"No. The doctor said he wants to keep you another day. At least," she answered, and he tugged on her arm until she sat on the edge of the bed. Then he pulled her again until she was lying next to him. He wrapped his arms around her and rested his forehead in the nape of her neck.

"There," he sighed. "Now, this is what I had planned. This and some really good food. Roasted wild turkey, which I hunted myself and made a point not to name." He heard her chuckle. "My mother's sweet potatoes and cranberry sauce. Mashed potatoes from my own garden. Stuffing. The whole works."

"That sounds good." He heard her stomach growl.

"Want some of my Jell-O?" he asked and heard her chuckle.

"No, they're bringing us both breakfast."

"Okay, then," he continued. "After eating, we were going to sit by the fire, open presents, and..." He shifted and tried to focus on her face. "Then I was going to propose to you."

He felt her stiffen for a brief moment, then she relaxed again.

"Oh? Is there a ring?" she asked, causing him to smile.

"It's wrapped and sitting under the tree," he assured her. "But you'll just have to figure out which box it's in. There are twenty of them under there for you."

"Twenty?" she gasped. "You bought me twenty presents?"

"I sure did." He relaxed back. "How many did you get me?"

She was quiet for a moment. "Four. No wait. Five. I added a last-minute present."

"Oh?" he asked, shifting until he was lying down a little more. He was suddenly more tired than hungry.

"Yes. You'll just have to wait and open all of them tomorrow. But first, you need to rest." She kissed him on the forehead as he drifted off to sleep.

CHAPTER NINETEEN

Kara watched Nick sleep and was thankful he couldn't see her. She was still a mess from last night. Liz was on her way with a change of clothing and some much-needed makeup to hide the bruises she'd gotten when Larry had kicked her and broken free.

Her cheek was a dark purple at the moment. She was even sporting a black eye. Her left hand was wrapped in gauze. She'd been assured the burn was minor, but the pain had caused her to ask for something to help dull the ache.

She hadn't eaten anything the night before, too afraid to take her eyes from Nick as he'd slept. Each time he opened his eyes, she was there, even if he wasn't really conscious.

Before he'd woken, Kyle had informed her that the barn fire was out, but the structure had burned completely to the ground, taking the chicken house with it. She hadn't wanted to ask if any of the hens had survived. She wasn't sure if Nick had put them up for the night, and she hoped that some of them got away.

Kyle had told her that Gobble and Giblets were alive

and that they, along with the rest of her animals, had been rounded up and moved to Nick's place.

She'd called her parents and had left them a message. Her mind hurt too much to try and calculate where they were or what time it was there.

Instead of telling them about the fire, she'd just left a message to have them call her when they could. She hadn't wanted to spoil their trip. Besides, what could they do that she wasn't already doing herself?

She had enough worry and anger to fuel herself through the worst of it. Especially after seeing the picture of Wilbert holding the bloodied sledgehammer.

When she heard a light knock on the door, she rolled away from Nick and opened the door for Liz.

"I brought—" Liz started, then she gasped and rushed to cup Kara's face in her hands. "Oh my god. You said you were bruised, you didn't say it was this bad."

"I did tell you I got kicked in the face by a horse," she joked. "This is what that looks like."

"Right." Liz frowned. "Okay, everything you need is in here." She lifted a bag. "Go clean up." She motioned to the bathroom. "I'll sit and watch over our hero."

"Thanks." She took the bag from Liz, but before disappearing into the bathroom, she hugged her friend. "Thanks," she said again.

She dropped the bag inside the bathroom, peeled off her ruined clothes, and tossed them in the trash can. Everything she was wearing was either ruined or smelled so bad of smoke, she didn't want to try to salvage it.

She'd already seen her reflection in the mirror several times, so she didn't bother looking again. Instead, she stepped into the small shower and let the lukewarm water wash away as much as she could. She was thankful she and

Liz used the same shampoo. The familiar scent warmed her and helped her relax even more.

Even though they were best friends, Liz was a great deal shorter than Kara, so the yoga pants she'd brought her hit her mid-calf. The baggy sweatshirt, however, was soft and exactly what she needed.

When she stepped out of the bathroom, Nick was sitting up and eating from a tray of food while Liz was chatting about what she'd gotten her parents for Christmas.

"Hey," she said, stepping beside Nick.

"Do you feel better?" Nick asked.

"Much." She sat beside him.

"Why didn't you tell me Larry kicked you?" His hand reached up to her face. "Is it bad?"

"No," she lied.

"Yes," Liz said. "She's purple. From the tip of her chin to the top of her cheekbone."

"Tattletale." She stuck her tongue out at her friend, who laughed.

"If I didn't tell him now, when he gets his vision back, he'd never trust anything I said again," Liz pointed out. "They brought you a tray of food too." She motioned to the tray on the table.

"Here." Nick moved over. "We can have breakfast together."

"Did you fill Liz in on what the police said and the photo?" she asked, settling beside Nick.

"Yes," Nick answered.

"My parents wouldn't even let me come here alone. They dropped me off in the lobby like I was in grade school." Liz rolled her eyes. "They're going to pick me up in an hour."

"Liz says there's a huge manhunt out for the four of them," Nick said.

"It's all over the news. Their mug shots are up there and everything." Liz motioned to the television. "Want to watch?"

"Sure, but let's keep the volume down," Nick answered.

For the next hour, they watched the news. There weren't really any new details. Some very grainy video of the shooting at the farmer's market. One shot in particular stopped on a grainy picture of what was obviously Willy running away from the gazebo area.

"We were standing about ten feet away from there." Liz visibly shivered.

"We got lucky he's such a bad shot," Nick joked.

"Too bad whoever it was that shot Rudy wasn't," Liz said softly.

"Yeah." Kara reached out for Liz's hand.

"I'm—" Liz started but then her phone chimed. After reading a text she sighed. "My folks are here to pick me up." She stood up, but then gasped lightly. "I forgot to give you both your presents." She rushed over to a large bag she'd dumped just inside the room and pulled out two small packages. "Here." She shoved one towards Kara and the other she set on Nick's lap.

"Do you want us to open them now?" Kara asked.

"Of course. I want all the joy of seeing your faces when you see..."—she winced as she looked at Nick's unfocused eyes—"find out what I got you both."

"I have yours back home. I was going to drop it off..." Kara said as she unwrapped the small blue box. Inside sat a small gold key. Kara pulled it out and held it up. "What?"

Liz smiled. "It's a key to your future. My parents have agreed to lease you the building next to Get Buzzed. If you want it. The place is yours to open your bakery." Liz squealed happily. "Which leads us to your gift, Nick. I didn't know what to get a man who has everything, so..."

Nick opened his box and inside was a piece of paper folded up.

"I... can't read this," he said.

Kara took it and unfolded it. "It's a promise agreement from the Food Mart to sell Florence's Jams in their store all throughout the state of Wyoming."

"Thanks." Nick smiled.

"It was the least I could do. Since my biggest gift is a head for business, I figured I'd put it to use," Liz said with a smile.

"Thank you." Kara walked over and hugged her friend.

"Your first order of business is to hire a good friend to help you set up the business. I just happen to know a gal for the job," Liz added.

Kara laughed. "I can't wait," she said, knowing it was the truth. She hadn't thought she would be excited, but she really was. Deep down in her heart, she'd wanted to jump at the chance of going into business. And thanks to Liz, she was. "Thank you," she said again as she hugged Liz. Liz's phone went off again, and her friend rolled her eyes.

"Okay, that's the second bell. If I don't go now, they'll come up after me," Liz joked. "Bye, Merry Christmas," she said as she rushed out.

"Are you happy?" Nick asked when she sat back down next to him.

"Very." She sighed. "You?"

"Very." He pulled her closer. "You never did answer me," he pointed out.

"About?" she asked, running her eyes over his and noticing his eyes were now focused on her face.

"Marrying me."

She smiled. "You haven't officially asked me. I hear there's a ring and all."

He chuckled. "Okay, we're going to play it this way?"

She laughed. "I guess so."

He pulled her into a hug. "Okay, until tomorrow then." He kissed her. "I've waited this long, what's one more day?"

At ten that night, the manhunt was still on for Nick's uncle and cousin. Mike and Dean had been taken into custody.

It was hard for either of them to fall asleep that night, so they stayed up and watched television as they held one another in the hospital bed. Nick's vision was back, for the most part. He was still having a difficult time reading but could see faces clearly.

By the next morning, even that had cleared up. A few hours later, they rode with Daryl in the truck back to Nick's place. The dogs were so excited to see them that it took almost ten minutes to get them to calm down.

Her parents finally called her once she and Nick had settled down to eat the pre-made meal Liz's mother had made for them as a thank-you for saving her daughter.

Even though it wasn't fresh caught free-range turkey and Nick's mother's recipes, it was still a wonderful Christmas meal.

"Merry Christmas, honey," her parents shouted.

She put them on speaker.

"Merry Christmas. Nick's here," she said quickly. "Where are you two?" she asked after hearing loud noise in the background.

"We're on the Eiffel Tower," her mother answered. "At the top."

"Wow, and you picked now to call us?" Kara joked.

"We just wanted to let you know we were thinking of you," her father said.

"Merry Christmas. Now, get off the phone and enjoy the view." Kara smiled.

"Will do. We'll talk later tonight," her mother added before the line went dead.

"You haven't told them about the barn yet, have you?" Nick asked.

"No." She shrugged. She hadn't even wanted to think about it. Not yet. "I don't want to worry them. Besides, what could they do? They'd probably cancel the rest of their trip or spend it worrying."

Nick nodded. "Okay, so let's finish eating so we can start a fire and open our presents."

She glanced towards his tree. "I had Daryl grab your presents from my place."

His eyes moved to the tree. "All of them?"

She shrugged. "Except one."

His eyebrows shot up. "I want to open that one first."

She laughed. "Not unless you tell me which one of those my ring is in." She pointed to all the boxes.

He shook his head. "Okay, so I'll wait."

She nodded. "I thought so."

Once both of their plates were empty, they moved into the living room. She started shaking each box under the tree with her name on it while he started the fire.

"That's cheating," he pointed out.

"You can't cheat when it comes to opening gifts."

"Oh? Then you won't mind if I..." He reached over and tore a bow off one of the presents she'd bought for him.

She laughed. "Go ahead."

He shifted and sat beside her, but instead of opening the box, he handed her one instead.

"Start with this one," he said.

She smiled and shook it lightly, causing him to laugh again. Then she tore off the red bow and the decorative paper.

Inside was a small blue box with a silver bracelet inside. The silver design looked older.

"It was my grandmother's," he pointed out. "It's a bangle. Or so my mother always called it. There's a really old engraving inside."

She turned the bracelet in her hands until the light from the fire made the words easy to read.

"My heart, my life, all for my love," she read out loud.

"The story goes that my grandfather gave it to my grandmother the night he proposed to her," he said with a smile.

"I see your theme going here." She felt her heart flutter while he reached over and slid the bracelet onto her right wrist.

"My turn," he said, pulling the box he'd started opening towards him.

She groaned. "It's a stupid—" she started, but he stopped her with a look.

"Whatever it is, I'm going to love it." He opened the box to the sweater she'd picked out.

"Okay, that's the worst gift I got you. I swear." She groaned.

He laughed as he pulled the sweater over his head. "I like it. Blue is my favorite color. It's the same color as your eyes." He reached over and took another box from under the tree, this one a little bigger than the last.

When she unwrapped a silver necklace, she frowned. "You didn't get me all jewelry, did you?"

He laughed. "No, there's a sweater or two in here for you as well."

She smiled. "Okay, what's the story with this one?" She held up the delicate chain as he helped her put it on. There was a small teardrop shape that dangled from the chain. "It's beautiful."

"Tears of my father the night my mother finally said yes," he said with a slight frown. "She left it for her future daughter-in-law. This present is really from her to you," he said, his eyes meeting hers.

She felt her heart skip. "I always liked your mother." She touched the tear shape. "I'll cherish it always."

He smiled. "Which one should I open next?"

She pointed to the bigger box and sat back to watch him open the new end table she'd purchased him. "There are four more like it in my garage. Daryl said he'd grab them tomorrow."

Nick set the new end table next to the sofa they had picked out together. "It matches so well."

She laughed and held out her hand for her next presents, which ended up being a deep red sweater, followed by a blue one. He'd also purchased her silver earrings that matched the teardrop necklace perfectly.

She had purchased him a few throw pillows for his new sofa and some curtains. Each time he opened a gift, he put the items she'd gotten for his home in place.

"We can hang the curtains tomorrow," he pointed out. "Now..." He pulled the last of her boxes from under the tree and held it up.

"Before that." She stood up. "I have to give you your last present." She took the box from his hands and, taking it with her, took his hand in hers and headed outside. "We'll need our coats and boots." She slipped into her boots and jacket while Nick pulled on his.

"What—" he started, but she gave him a look and he chuckled. "Lead the way." He motioned after opening the door.

When they stepped into the barn, she was thankful to see all of her animals safely tucked inside. She ran her hands over each of her horses' heads and stopped just outside of the last stall.

When Nick saw the bow tied around Wilbur's neck, he laughed. "You gave me a pig?"

She smiled. "Yes, I gave you a pig. One that you never have to eat and can continue spoiling for the rest of his life."

Nick wrapped his arms around her. "This is the best gift I have ever gotten."

She laughed. "The bar is set pretty low then."

"Now, open your last gift." He motioned to the box. "Here, now, in front of our animals." He nodded towards Wilbur.

As she peeled the soft blue paper away from the box, Nick slowly slid down to one knee on the cement floor.

When she opened the box, she felt tears burn her eyes as she looked down at his mother's ring. She remembered commenting on the unique design when she'd seen his mother wearing it all those years ago.

The heart-shaped diamond and solid white gold band had impressed the young Kara. Now, with the ring glimmering in the soft light from the barn, Kara's heart melted.

"Kara," Nick said, taking her hand and slipping the ring onto her finger, "you know how I feel about you. You're my universe. My world. I can't imagine being anywhere without you. If everything went up in smoke tomorrow, the only thing that would matter was that you were by my side."

He kissed her knuckles softly. "Marry me. Make a life with me. Wherever we chose to be."

Kara knelt down and wrapped her arms around him. "Yes," she said softly. "I love you, Nick."

"Well, well, isn't this a sight for sore eyes." Wilbert stepped out from the shadows of the barn just as Willy stepped through the barn doors. Both men held guns aimed directly at them.

CHAPTER TWENTY

Nick's entire body went on guard. If he and Kara hadn't been kneeling on the cement floor, he would have shoved her body behind his. As it was, he didn't dare make any sudden moves. He didn't trust his uncle or his cousin not to just shoot them right then.

"What do you want?" he asked, holding up his hands. Kara did the same, slowly.

"What do we want?" Willy laughed. "Everything you have." He rushed over and yanked the ring from Kara's fingers as she cried out. "Starting with this." He held up the ring.

"That was my mother's," Nick hissed.

"Which was bought with Howe money. Money stolen from my daddy by yours," Wilbert yelled.

"This too." Willy reached for the bracelet Kara was wearing. "That was my grandmother's," Willy said, fighting to get it from Kara's wrist.

"You can't expect to steal the ranch from us," Nick pointed out. "I've filed my will. If anything happens to us, everything goes to Daryl."

Wilbert laughed. "You have no authority. You see, my brother's will stated that if you weren't married by Christmas Day, which is today, then I get everything."

Nick tensed. "That isn't..." He shook his head. "That's not..."

"That can't be right," Kara finished for him.

"Oh, but it is. When my brother's lawyer gets here, he'll confirm it all." Wilbert looked down at his watch. "When that happens, I'll have you both arrested for trespassing."

"We'll see how you like that." Willy laughed and started dancing around the barn. "I think I'll start by shooting this here pig." He pointed the gun at Wilbur and Nick felt his anger grow.

"He's not yours yet," Nick said, standing up and pulling Kara to her feet, making sure to put her body behind his.

Willy's gun moved to them, but Wilbert stopped him.

"No, not until we hear the reading of the will." He glanced at his watch again. "Where is that damn lawyer?"

"You know that Stephen is supposed to be here?" Nick asked, confused. The man had agreed to stop by sometime before five that evening to officially read his father's will. He'd lost track of time and didn't even know what time it was now.

"Of course, I do." Wilbert laughed. "I know everything that goes on in my town."

"Then you know who broke into Nick's house and destroyed everything?" Kara asked firmly.

"Of course, I do," Wilbert hissed. "As I said, I know everything that goes on here. My son was pissed that you got his friends in trouble at the Firehouse. They were just going to show that slut friend of yours a good time. Everyone in town knows she's nothing more than whore." Wilbert laughed. "Paybacks. Besides, all that shit your mother put in the house was trash anyway. She never did have any style. My Marge has better taste in her sleep than your mother ever had."

Nick felt his anger grow, but Kara held his hand firmly and kept him back.

"What about attacking Nick and burning my barn? That isn't your property," she pointed out.

"Nick deserved it. I had hoped they'd discover his body and blame him for the fire. Too bad he woke up and you returned when you did," Wilbert said with a chuckle.

"You just confessed to trying to kill me?" Nick growled. "And you think they'd let you keep the ranch?"

"Course they will." Wilbert's smile doubled. "A man has a right to defend his property against two thieves." He lifted his gun and aimed it directly at Nick's heart.

Just then, they all heard a car in the driveway. Wilbert and Willy turned towards the sound, and Nick took that moment of distraction to yank open the door to Wilbur's stall. The pig didn't disappoint and rushed towards Wilbert, taking his uncle to the ground. The man's gun went sliding across the cement floor and landed at Kara's feet.

Willy yelled and rushed to help his father just as Kara picked up the gun. Then, as if sensing his mistake, Willy turned towards Nick, his gun circling around with him as Kara lifted Wilbert's gun and shot two bullets into Willy.

Willy cried out as his gun hit the ground. He fell directly next to Wilbert, in a heap. Wilbert was still trying to fight off an angry three-hundred-pound pig.

Suddenly, there was a lot of shouting as five police officers rushed into the barn, guns aimed at Wilbert and Willy.

"Wilbur." Nick snapped his fingers and the pig turned away from his uncle and went back into his pen. "Good boy." He grabbed an apple from a bucket and gave it to the pig. Nick turned to Kara, who had handed his uncle's gun over to Kyle. "Like I said, best present ever," he said as he wrapped his arms around her.

"I love you," Kara said in a shaky tone.

"I love you too."

Then, to his surprise, she walked over to Willy, who was writhing in pain, and yanked the ring and bracelet from his hands. Then she stepped over Willy and put both of them back into his hands. "Give them to me again. This time, I promise I'll never let anyone take them from me again."

He smiled as he slid first the bracelet and then the ring back on her.

"Marry me?" he asked again.

"Yes," she said and kissed him.

"You are one incredible woman." He took her hand in his.

"He was going to shoot you. I'm sure that once all the adrenaline wears off, I'll freak out. But for now, I know I did the right thing."

Nick nodded. "I agree." He turned to Kyle. "I assume Stephen called you?"

"He didn't have to. Daryl spotted your uncle and Willy sneaking onto the property and called it in. Stephen's up at the house though, waiting for you. Why don't you head on up, and we'll clean this mess up."

From what they could see, Kara had shot Willy in the leg. They didn't even care if both bullets had hit him or if he was going to be okay.

They made their way back to the house, where Daryl and Stephen were waiting in the living room.

"Are the two of you all right?" Daryl asked, rushing to them.

"Yes," Nick answered and hugged the man. "Thanks to you."

Daryl nodded. "Just... doing my job."

Nick laughed. "Daryl, we both know you're more than just an employee. You're family." He hugged him again. Then Kara walked over and gave the man a hug too.

"Good, everyone is here," Stephen said, getting their attention. "I think it's time we got this done." He walked over to sit at the table. The three of them sat down as well.

"I won't bore you with the boring stuff," Stephen said over his glasses as he pulled out a folder. Then he handed an envelope to each of them. "Personalized letters to each of you from Nicholas."

Kara frowned down at her envelope. "I have one too?"

Stephen nodded. He motioned to her left hand. "I see that you've completed the last requirement placed by your father before his death, which means..."—he put the folder back in his briefcase and pulled out another one—"this is the will I'll be reading tonight."

"Wait." Nick held up his hands as he looked between every face there. "Seriously? My father had two wills. If I hadn't asked Kara to marry me, I wouldn't have gotten the farm?"

"No, not all of it." Stephen sat back. "If you two had not gotten engaged, you would have gotten half, and Kara would have gotten the other half." Stephen smiled.

"So..." he said slowly, "my uncle wouldn't have gotten it either way?"

"Nope." Stephen shook his head. "Daryl still gets his land, no matter what." He motioned to Daryl. "The ranch house and five acres, including the barn, are all yours." He slid over a thick envelope. "The deed, free and clear."

Daryl smiled and held the envelope to his heart. "Bless that fool." He shook his head. "Thank you."

"For you two." Stephen slid them another thick envelope. "Once it's official, you can change the name on the deed. For now, this place is yours. Congratulations, by the way." He motioned to the ring on Kara's finger. "We, your father and I, knew the two of you had it coming." He chuckled. "We just doubted if you'd do it on your own without a little nudge." He stood up. "Now, I'm going to go home and eat the rest of my turkey dinner. Merry Christmas." He slapped Daryl on the shoulder. "Walk me out?"

The pair walked out the front door just as Kyle knocked on the back one. All three dogs happily barked and danced around as the man gave them his attention briefly.

"Well?" Nick asked.

"The paramedics have Willy, and we've got your uncle," Kyle said as he straightened.

"Oh," Kara said, pulling out her cell phone. Nick heard a quick woosh sound as a file was sent to Kyle's phone.

"Wilbert's confession. Sorry if it's a little muffled. My phone was in my pocket," she said with a smile.

"Damn." Kyle shook his head as he hit play on the file. They listened as Wilbert clearly confessed to knowing everything that went on in his town. "Well, this will help. Not sure if the courts will like it, but..." He smiled. "It helps. We'll get out of your way. I just wanted you to know that they won't be bothering you again. Not for a long time." Kyle shook Nick's hand. "Congratulations on the engagement." He motioned to Kara. "We all were rooting for you two."

Nick laughed and wrapped his arm around Kara. "Thanks."

"Merry Christmas." Kyle nodded.

"You, too," Kara and he said at the same time.

They stood on the front porch and watched the police cruisers disappear in the distance.

"Well? What are we going to do now?" Kara asked him as she wrapped her arms around him a little tighter. "It's going to be boring around here without being shot at, hit over the head, burned, and... well, shot at again." She sighed.

He smiled down at her. "I can think of a couple things that can keep us busy and entertained. If you like living dangerously."

"Oh?" she asked, her eyebrows going up.

He chuckled. "Sure. How do you feel about kids?"

EPILOGUE

With the logs crackling in the fireplace, Nick and Kara opened their individual letters from his father later that night.

After reading each of them quietly to themselves, they read them out loud to one another.

"*Son,*

I'm so proud of the man you've become. I wish your mother and I could be around to see you continue to grow. To enjoy seeing you start your own family. I now you always hated my antics, but I hope this last one proves to be worth it. From the day you came back home complaining about the new girl that moved in next door, your mother and I knew that, someday, Kara would be part of our family. I'm just happy you didn't wait forever like I did.

With all my heart,

Your father"

Nick's eyes were so wet it was almost impossible to see his father's signature at the bottom. Then Kara read her note.

"Kara, my dear, hopefully my soon-to-be daughter,

You may not have seen Nick's mother and I watching you from the moment you moved in next door, but we were there, watching you bloom into the amazing, kind woman you are today. I wish Florence could be here to see your joy when Nick slipped her ring onto your finger. Just know that she always thought of you as the daughter we never could have.

When your folks and I came up with the plan to get the two of you together, I never imagined it would work out so well. Seeing my son's face each day when he returned from your ranch, I knew he was long gone in love with you long before he did.

Welcome to the family,

Nicholas.

P.S. Feel free to name your first born after me. It's sort of a tradition."

"I can't believe my parents were in on this. That they had been planning it all along with your dad," Kara said after reading the note.

"I think Liz was right," Nick said, pulling her close to his side again. "I think the entire town knew about us long before we did."

She smiled. "So, the last question I have is..." She looked up at him. "Just how many kids were you thinking of having?"

"Well, we have four empty bedrooms." He brushed his lips across hers. "But I could always add more to the house."

She laughed. "When do you want to get started on that family?" she purred as he pulled her over him.

He kissed her. "How about right now?"

ALSO BY JILL SANDERS

The Pride Series

Finding Pride

Discovering Pride

Returning Pride

Lasting Pride

Serving Pride

Red Hot Christmas

My Sweet Valentine

Return To Me

Rescue Me

A Pride Christmas

The Secret Series

Secret Seduction

Secret Pleasure

Secret Guardian

Secret Passions

Secret Identity

Secret Sauce

Secret Obsession

Secret Desire

Secret Charm

Secret Santa

The West Series

Loving Lauren

Taming Alex

Holding Haley

Missy's Moment

Breaking Travis

Roping Ryan

Wild Bride

Corey's Catch

Tessa's Turn

Saving Trace

Christmas Holly

Maggie's Match

The Grayton Series

Last Resort

Someday Beach

Rip Current

In Too Deep

Swept Away

High Tide

Sunset Dreams

Lucky Series

Unlucky In Love

Sweet Resolve

Best of Luck

A Little Luck

Christmas Wish

Silver Cove Series

Silver Lining

French Kiss

Happy Accident

Hidden Charm

A Silver Cove Christmas

Sweet Surrender

Second Chances

Entangled Series – Paranormal Romance

The Awakening

The Beckoning

The Ascension

The Presence

The Calling

The Chosen

The Beyond

Haven, Montana Series

Closer to You

Never Let Go

Holding On

Coming Home

The Hard Way

Pride Oregon Series

A Dash of Love

My Kind of Love

Season of Love

Tis the Season

Dare to Love

Where I Belong

Because of Love

A Thing Called Love

First Comes Love

Someone to Love

Fools in Love

FindingLove

Wildflowers Series

Summer Nights

Summer Heat

Summer Secrets

Summer Fling

Summer's End

Summer Wish

Summer Breeze

Summer Ride

Distracted Series

Wake Me

Tame Me

Save Me

Dare Me

Stand Alone Books

Twisted Rock

Hope Harbor

Raven Falls

Angel Bluff

Day Break

For a complete list of books:

http://JillSanders.com

ABOUT THE AUTHOR

Jill Sanders is a New York Times, USA Today, and international bestselling author of Sweet Contemporary Romance, Romantic Suspense, Western Romance, and Paranormal Romance novels. With over 85 books in eleven series, translations into several different languages, and audiobooks there's plenty to choose from. Look for Jill's bestselling stories wherever romance books are sold or visit her at jillsanders.com

Jill comes from a large family with six siblings, including an identical twin. She was raised in the Pacific Northwest and later relocated to Colorado for college and a successful IT career before discovering her talent for writing sweet and sexy page-turners. After Colorado, she decided to move south, living in Texas and now making her home along the Emerald Coast of Florida. You will find that the settings of several of her series are inspired by her time spent living in these areas. She has two sons and off-set the testosterone in her house by adopting three furry little ladies that provide her company while she's locked in her writing cave. She enjoys heading to the beach, hiking, swimming, wine-tasting, and pickleball with her husband, and of course writing. If you have read any of her books, you may also notice that there is a love of food, especially sweets! She has been blamed for a few added pounds by her assistant, editor, and fans... donuts or pie anyone?

- facebook.com/JillSandersBooks
- twitter.com/JillMSanders
- amazon.com/Jill-Sanders/e/B009M2NFD6?tag=jillm-com-20
- bookbub.com/authors/jill-sanders
- instagram.com/jillsandersauthor